MW01134335

A Heart That Forgives

Beverly Taylor

No part of this book may be reproduced, stored in a retrieval system, or transmitted by any means without the written permission of the author.

ISBN- 9781797584652

The views expressed in this work are solely those of the author and do not necessarily reflect the views of the publisher, and the publisher hereby disclaims any responsibility for them.

©2019 by Beverly Taylor All rights reserved.

In loving memory of my parents, Hugh Taylor, Jr. and Johnnie Mae Taylor; my brother, Dewey A. Taylor; my sister, Alesia Y. Taylor; my niece, Fanisha C. Collins; and my nephews, David Taylor-Savare and Zachary E. Franklin.

Rest well until we meet again.

Chapter One

Ten years ago, Dannielle (Danni) Wright, was born to Pastor Wallie Allen and Rosie Mae Wright. From the day she was born, she adored her daddy. He adored and loved his only baby girl. Danni could do no wrong in his eyes and she knew it. She was spoiled, but she wasn't a brat. Danni's mom would tell her dad that Danni wasn't obeying and not listening to her, but he would make excuses for Danni because he loved her so much. It hurt him to see her disciplined. Looking at Danni was like looking in the mirror for her father. They looked exactly alike; she even had his outgoing personality. They both had slanted eyes, high cheek bones, and caramel-colored flawless skin. They also had the same-shaped birthmark on their scalps, in the exact same place. Having Danni was one of his greatest gifts. He'd never loved anyone as much as he loved her. Danni could draw a crowd by singing or dancing. He knew she would be amazing in ministry, because she already showed signs of being a great singer, preacher, and leader at a very young age.

Pastor Wright knew his daughter would be self-driven and curious about things in life. She refused to ask for guidance and had to figure things out herself; eventually, it would cause her to be disciplined. He even thought that because of her many adventurous occurrences, maybe she needed a sibling. So, he and Rosie discussed it. They agreed they could handle another child, but secretly prayed the child would be much calmer than Danni.

With many enjoyable afternoon and nights, it didn't take long for Rosie to conceive. They were excited about the pregnancy. After sharing the news of the baby, Danni made it very clear she wanted a brother. She would talk to her mother's growing belly and refer to the baby as *him*. Pastor Wright wanted a son as well, but he would be just as happy with another daughter, as long as she was healthy. Danni would rub her mom's stomach daily and talk to her baby brother. Every night, she would pray with him and tell him she loved him.

Rosie had always been spoiled by her husband, from the love he shared with her to the best material things money could buy. While pregnant, he was excessively attentive to her and her cravings. He would make store runs in the wee hour of the mornings for chocolate candy bars, Cheez-It crackers, and she would wash them down with

Coca-Cola. He hired a live-in assistant to help her, prevent her from being stressed, and to be with her while he was at work.

He loved seeing her pregnant. Rosie wanted to know the gender, but he convinced her to wait and enjoy the surprise. Rosie knew if she really wanted to know, he would go along with it, however. He believed he was having a son and had picked out the name, Wallie Allen Wright, III. His nickname would be Dubb. Their love was genuine and beautiful. They were true soulmates.

The phone rang, and Rosie answered. It was Bishop Taylor for her husband. Rosie explained he was not in and took a message for him. After her husband returned home, she told him about the phone call. Pastor Wright was nervous about why Bishop Taylor called him. He returned his phone call and learned that he was being elevated to a bishop. He felt so unworthy of the elevation. Rosie explained to him how he had been a blessing to the community and always gave back to other ministries. He was an amazing pastor loved by all.

During Rosie's last month of pregnancy, her husband would be consecrated as a Bishop. Most of the members of the General Board of the Pentecostal of the Apostolic Faith of Jesus Christ, Inc. voted to elevate him over the newly created Northern California Jurisdiction. The Presiding Bishop, Hugh Taylor, had requested to hold the installation service at Pastor Wright's church, Greater St. Luke Apostolic Worship Center. The church could seat well over 10,000 and another 200 in each overflow room. Bishop Taylor scheduled the service three weeks away. Pastor Wallie, Rosie, and a team of supporters planned the service and a dinner to follow. The members of his church were ecstatic for their pastor.

Not much would change in the sanctuary, as it was already beautifully decorated with lined purple chairs in a half-circular pattern and beige carpet with a large gold pulpit in the middle of the sanctuary. The banquet center unattached to the church was decorated in royal colors—purple and gold. They decorated tables with huge, glass centerpieces full of a large bouquet of purple roses, dripping with baby's breath and silver-dollar eucalyptus greens in each. The team was extremely excited about the celebration.

As the day approached, Pastor Wright was concerned about his wife. She had been involved and working diligently in the planning of the installation service. She had the perfect eye for decorating. She was the one who had the vision for the sanctuary and turned it into the beautiful edifice it was. He noticed her feet were swollen and she was walking much slower than usual. He wanted her to go home and rest. She walked by his office and he called her; she stopped in her tracks to see what he wanted. He stood to meet her halfway, held her, and told her she had done enough work. He called for the car to take her home. Rosie could be stubborn at times, but she knew she was tired and needed rest.

Later that night as she slept, a sharp pain woke her up. She sat up and rubbed her stomach. The pain subsided, so she laid back down. In ten minutes, she felt the same horrendous pain and noticed it lasted almost a minute. She began to pray, because she wasn't due for another three weeks. The next atrocious pain hit her in seven minutes. She tried to stand up, but she couldn't. She instructed her assistant to call her husband; she got no answer, so she left a voice mail. She remembered her husband and Danni were at the church finalizing everything before tomorrow's celebration. Although she wanted to meet her baby, she didn't want to meet him tonight, as the installation service was scheduled for the next day. Another unbearable pain hit her hard and she cried out. Her assistant ran to her, grabbed her bag, and helped her to the car.

At the hospital, her assistant called her husband to let him know she had been admitted to Santa Barbara Cottage Hospital. He could hear Rosie moan in pain as another contraction battered her body. She refused any medication. The nurse insisted she accept the epidural to help ease the pain. As the contractions came, Rosie's blood pressure rose to dangerous levels. The nurse said she had preeclampsia, and they had to deliver the baby immediately through caesarian section or else the baby would be at risk. Rosie wanted to wait until her husband arrived, but the nurse said the doctors were waiting for her in the delivery room. Rosie was upset; she wanted her husband and Danni with her. She prayed before they medicated her. She remembered counting down from a hundred, and then waking up to the sound of a crying baby.

The doctor said, "Mrs. Wright, it's a boy!"

Rosie cried and smiled at the same time. She knew her husband wanted a son and Danni wanted a brother. God had answered their prayers.

Pastor Wallie and Danni were pacing in the waiting room. The nurse asked for the Wright family members. Pastor Wallie looked nervous, knowing it was too early to have the baby. She told them they had a new son and brother. Danni started jumping up and down while Pastor

Wallie smiled. He wanted to see them. The nurse escorted them into Rosie's room. She laid there with a huge smile on her face. The baby had been taken away to get cleaned and undergo routine tests. Pastor Wallie kissed her and apologized for not being with her when she had delivered their son. She loved him and explained to him she knew he wanted to be there; however, with her blood pressure rising, they wanted to make sure he was not in any danger. They had to take him immediately. He noticed she looked tired, but he figured that was normal for someone who had just went through surgery. Danni kissed her mom, but she wanted to see her brother. The nurse walked in rolling a portable bassinet. Danni walked with the nurse and observed her brother crying.

"He looks like me," Danni yelled.

Pastor Wallie picked up his son with tears in his eyes. He looked at Rosie and bent over and kissed her again.

Wallie Allen Wright, III, nicknamed Dubb, was born on August 13th, after a trouble-free pregnancy. He was gorgeous with a lovely head of dark, straight hair and weighed a healthy nine pounds and eight ounces; he was twenty-four inches long. He looked like Danni did when she was born, but she was much heavier and longer.

Because Rosie had gone into labor early, she missed the installation service. The newly appointed Bishop Wallie Wright told her every single detail. She was so sad she had missed it for him, but she was glad to have delivered her beautiful son.

Rosie was released from the hospital three days after delivering Dubb. Her husband, Danni, and her assistants helped with the new baby. He woke up every hour on the hour for a feeding and diaper change. Baby Dubb brought more joy to their house. When Danni got home from school, she ran up the stairs to be with her brother. She took care of him like he was hers. She adored her little brother.

One chilly night, Bishop Wallie woke up and realized Dubb hadn't awakened him. Rosie told him she would check on him, but Bishop Wallie told her to go back to sleep. He would change and feed him. He walked in the room and Dubb's face was blue. He yelled out for Rosie to call 911. Dubb wasn't breathing. Rosie was screaming, which woke up Danni. Danni looked like a deer in headlights. She couldn't say anything, nor could she move. Rosie was administering CPR as Bishop Wallie prayed out loud. Rosie cried as she continued to administer CPR.

"He's not breathing," she yelled. His skin was blue and cold. One of Rosie's assistants tried to grab Danni's hand to take her away, but Danni snatched her hand back; she had to be there. She had to see her brother breathe again and know he was going to be okay. The paramedics arrived. One took over administering CPR. Dubb was hooked up to an electrocardiogram machine to monitor his heart rate, but there was none. They put him in the ambulance and rushed him to Children's Hospital. Fear gripped Rosie, Wallie, and Danni.

Wallie prayed out loud as they jumped into their car to follow the ambulance. He began to speak life into Dubb from afar.

They finally reached the hospital. Wallie held onto Rosie and Danni's hands tightly. They didn't have time to check in as the doctor came out asking for the family of Wallie Wright III. The doctor explained to Wallie and Rose that they had done everything they could do to resuscitate him, but he did not respond. Their beautiful baby boy was gone.

Charles Cox was Danni's best friend. He was a bright young man. They had grown up together in Isla Vista, California, where they attended the same schools. He lived five blocks from her. They were always together, spending countless hours at each other's homes and sharing gossip or other information. Danni knew Charles' family well and Charles knew Danni's family well; however, he felt Danni's mother knew he had a crush on Danni and wasn't happy about it.

Charles and his family attended the memorial service. He'd never seen Danni so broken and hurt. He attempted to console her when she cried aloud, but his mother stopped him, because she was with her family— right where she belonged. He wanted to hug her, but he couldn't get to her. His mother held onto him, so he wouldn't be out of sync. He watched Danni the entire service. A woman started singing a song and Danni cried so uncontrollably that her father literally picked her motionless body up and carried her out of the church. When they walked by him, he called out to her, but she didn't respond. Danni's mother followed closely behind them. He made a quick move to leave his seat and be with Danni, but his mother stopped him again. At this point, he was furious and all he could do is weep for Danni.

Chapter Two

Several weeks later, Danni was back at Charles' house as usual, playing Super Mario Brothers on his Nintendo. She didn't mention anything about her brother's death or how she was feeling, so he didn't bring it up either. She told him she had missed him; he immediately hugged her and kissed her cheek. She giggled and pushed him away. Charles knew one day he was going to marry her.

He and Danni were laughing and talking about their normal everyday interests. She invited him to church again. He normally declined her invitations; however, because of what she was going through, he accepted her invitation. She was shocked, because he usually argued with her on the subject matter. Because of the passing of her brother, however, he wanted to try and make her happy. Even if it was just for a few minutes, he agreed to attend. He was always apprehensive about attending her church, because he had heard people catch the Holy Spirit and he was not going to let that happen to him.

Charles' family followed the Episcopal faith. At Charles' church, they sing hymnals from hymn books collectively and the priest delivered a sermon. The Sunday he attended Danni's church, he enjoyed the energy and the electrifying songs that were sang. Danni didn't tell him she was singing a solo before her father preached.

Bishop Wright introduced Danni before she sang. As she started to sing, Charles' mouth flew open; he was in shock. He knew Danni liked to sing gospel songs, but he had no idea Danni sang so well. He smiled the entire time she sang and became emotional. She sounded like an angel. When she finished singing, she took her seat next to him. He hugged her and told her that her voice gave him chills. They both smiled.

Charles sat attentively while Bishop Wright spoke and felt God was talking directly to him. Bishop Wright read the scripture text taken from Jeremiah 1:4-9 (King James Version):

Then the word of the Lord came unto me saying, Before I formed thee in the belly I knew thee; and before thou camest forth out of the womb I sanctified thee, and I ordained thee a prophet unto the nations, Then, said I, oh Lord God! Behold I cannot speak: for I am a child. But the Lord said unto me, say not, I am a child: for thou shalt go to all that I shall send thee, and whatsoever I command thee, and whatsoever I command thee thou shalt speak. Be not afraid of their faces; for I am with thee to deliver thee, said the Lord. Then the Lord put forth his hand and touched my mouth. And the Lord said unto me, Behold, I have put my words in thy mouth. See I have this day set thee over the nations and over the kingdoms, to root out, and to pull down, and to destroy, and to throw down, to build, and to plant.

Charles was amazed by the scripture text. The Word of the Lord had come alive in him. He felt surrounded by something peaceful. He wasn't afraid, but it was something he'd never felt before.

"Whatever this is…feels good," Charles said.

She smiled and whispered to him. "What you feel is the presence of God."

He returned the smile.

Bishop Wright declared, "You are a child of the King and He will take care of you."

Charles listened intently. Bishop Wright gave the invitation for anyone who wanted to give their life to Christ, desired prayer, or wanted to join the church to come forward. Charles released Danni's hand, and with tears streaming down his face, he walked toward Bishop. The

13

audience rejoiced by applauding him for making the decision to follow Christ. Bishop hugged Charles, had him repeat the prayer of repentance, and prepared him for baptism in Jesus' Name. Bishop Wright welcomed him into the church family.

On that day, Charles converted to Christianity. He loved his new church and the freshness of being a new Christian. He enjoyed bible study and Sunday services. He developed such a hunger for God's Word, and his character quickly changed for the better. Charles used to smoke weed with his friends, but since giving his life to Christ, he no longer desired to do so.

Years later, when they attended high school, Charles and Danni grew even closer and began dating. They had expressed their true love for each other and were officially a young couple. One afternoon, Charles saw Danni walking with her friends to the library. Just looking at her made his heart beat faster. He loved her. He followed her into the library, walked behind her, and kissed her neck. She yelped, because she didn't know who it was. When she turned around and saw him, she smiled. He opened his mouth and leaned into her mouth. She opened her mouth and their tongues tried to find purpose together. Charles held her close to his body while they continued their first passionate kiss. They were interrupted by the librarian clearing her throat loudly.

Charles and Danni's feelings flourished. Danni's mother wasn't too worried, because they were graduating from high school in a few months. Danni's dad was so proud of her accomplishments in school. She carried a 4.0 grade point average, which kept her on the honor roll. She was the Student Council President and President of the Debate Team. She was entered in the Who's Who among American High School Students and the National Honor Society and she was Valedictorian. She'd been offered many scholarships; however, her parents declined them since they were able to afford college.

Her father also knew she was too stubborn to listen to good advice about Charles. She had to find out for herself. Bishop Wright told his wife that when Charles hurt Danni, they would be there for her. "Once she submits her stubbornness to God, she'll be okay," he would tell her.

Danni was accepted to Harvard University in Massachusetts, and Charles was headed to Arizona State University, where he'd received a full scholarship to attend and play football. Danni's mom hoped the distance would affect their relationship and they would go their separate ways. She didn't believe Charles was good enough for her baby girl. There was something sneaky about him, and Danni would not listen. Her mother prayed that God would show her sweet baby that he was a no-good boy that would grow into a no-good man.

Danni was gifted in song, prophecy, and knowledge, and she could preach. Her preaching style almost reminded Rosie of her husband. She knew if Danni continued living for God and didn't let Charles sabotage her walk with Christ, she would have an amazing ministry.

Chapter Three

High school graduation was two weeks away. Mother Wright prepared Danni for the senior prom. She wasn't happy about Charles being her daughter's date; however, she went along with it as best as she could. Danni's father was amazed at how beautiful his daughter looked. She looked so much like him. He'd prayed for his daughter daily since she was born, asking God to protect her from the tricks of the enemy and to keep her mentally sane, so she could make good decisions.

Charles and Danni left for prom in all white and silver. She looked like an angel. Mother Wright cried at how beautiful her daughter was and realized she was growing up. She looked like a female version of her handsome father.

She looked at her husband and laid her head on his chest.

He held her and told her again, "Danni is a smart girl, and we've taught her how to use good judgment and make sound decisions. We must trust her, but not Charles."

They both laughed. He grabbed her hand and led her upstairs to their bedroom. He was feeling frisky, and he closed the door behind them.

It was time to present the king and queen the senior class had voted upon. There were four couples nominated. This was the most exciting time of prom. One of the teachers was on stage to announce the class king and queen. Danni was extremely nervous, causing her hands to sweat. Charles was more confident of their win than Danni was. The announcement was made, and they had won! They had dated for four years and were completely excited when they were selected. The happy couple proceeded to take the stage together with the roaring sound of applause from the crowd of students present. Charles was crowned with the honorary king's crown and the prom king sash, while Danni was presented with the queen tiara and the prom queen sash. The voters also saw admirable qualities in the couple as they made their opinion that Charles and Danni would be together forever. The school played an old-school Luther Vandross song. They slow danced the entire song. "I love you," Charles whispered in her ear. She laid her head on his chest and smiled.

Prom night was magical for Danni. Days afterward, she was still glowing. Floating on cloud nine, graduation day crept up on her. Danni was the Valedictorian at the Christian High School (CHS) graduation. There was an overwhelming excitement with the seniors of CHS. The amount of emotion felt on this day was unbelievable. There was a nervous feeling about graduating, because it was the beginning of a new journey. You could feel the excitement in the air. Danni's best friend, Ashlee, had always been there for her, through the good and the bad. She had spent a lot of time with Danni after her brother passed away. It was Ashlee who Danni cried to and spoke about Dubb. Ashlee lived next door to Danni and they were best friends until Danni started hanging around Charles. She didn't care for Charles at all and had talked to Danni many times about him, but Danni wouldn't listen. Danni would get angry at her for bringing up Charles negatively, so Ashlee decided to pretend to go along with their relationship, just so she and Danni could continue to be friends.

There were only 350 graduates; this means they'd gotten to know each other and considered themselves family. Danni had a way with words. They teased Danni about being a millennial activist and preacher. She always laughed at them and denied being a preacher or an advocate. She was nervous about graduation, because she had to prepare a speech to encourage her class as they embarked on a new journey. Danni and Ashlee prayed and asked God to give her what to say to their classmates.

The night before graduation, Danni was able to pull all her thoughts together and write her speech. She tested it on Ashlee. Ashlee was astonished by her best friend's wisdom and relationship with Christ. Danni was the one who had led her to Christ, and she would always be grateful to her.

At graduation, Danni wore an all-white cap and gown. She gave honor to God for helping her make it this far while learning how to grow up after experiencing her brother's death at an early age. Her parents cried knowing the pain, heartache, and suffering they had experienced after losing their son. They listened as Danni spoke.

"We have been looked after and protected by our families and teachers. Now, we prepare for the real world. We will face new temptations and new challenges. It is now between God and us. Our society today will encourage infidelity, lying, cheating, and substance abuse. Self-centeredness will be the dominant viewpoint.

For those of us who are continuing our education, I challenge you to be different. Christian groups too often say they are Christians, but they don't always walk in His steps, which makes us sound religious but not spiritual. They see Christianity as just obeying the big rules instead of a daily faith relationship with God. They might even ask you to do subtle things that break God's commandments. Take that extra step and honestly be Christ-like. Be the one person that everyone can look up to and say that you have the love of Jesus in your heart. Show them that you are truly on fire for God.

There will be places we go that will be hostile. Stand up for what you believe in. Stand up for God! This means you can't be afraid to say no. Remember, we will all have temptation, but we don't have to yield to it.

Where do you want to be at our ten-year class reunion? What do you want your life to say? Do you want your life to say I don't care about God and His laws? His laws are boring and don't really apply? It's just been so much fun out there partying, drinking, and using drugs? If this is what your life will say, you will be empty and unhappy. I want to say right now that 'I am on fire for God and wherever He leads me, I'm going to follow.' I recognize God, even through the death of my brother at ten days old. The many times I fed him, changed his diapers, kissed him, my brother knew me. He knew I loved him. God showed me He is my comforter. He is whatever we need Him to be in our lives. There is nothing to little He can't be for us, or too great. He is our Savior, our healer, and our deliverer. Why would we not serve a God like Him? He is alive!"

Danni's dad stood the entire time she spoke, but when she got to the end of her speech, he knew what her assignment was in life from God. Just the same as him, she was called to spread the Gospel of Jesus Christ. Everyone was standing, crying, applauding, shouting, and thanking God. It took them a while to settle down, so she could finish. Danni knew God wanted her to do something for Him but was unsure as to exactly what her calling was, until now!

Chapter Four

It was time for Danni and Charles' departure to their respective colleges. They went to dinner and hung out at Camino Del Sur Beach after eating. Charles kissed Danni and told her how much he loved her. While in the car, Charles continued to kiss Danni passionately. He reached under her shirt and squeezed her breasts. Things were getting heated, so she stopped him. He told her he wanted to make love to her. She explained over and over she wasn't ready for that, not until they're married. Charles told her they would get married after college. He argued as much as he could, but Danni couldn't be swayed. He eventually took her home and they talked all night and fell asleep on the phone. Before they fell asleep, he told her that he loved her. She told him she loved him, too.

During the first semester in college, Danni and Charles talked, texted, and video chatted with each other several times a day; however, when football season started, Danni noticed his calls tapered off. She would call him, and her phone calls would go directly to voicemail. Although she knew his schedule would be hectic with classes and

23

football, she didn't think she would have to go three days without hearing from him. She was furious. Once, she even called him at 3:00am and he should have answered, but he didn't. Danni was tired of calling and texting him and not getting a response. After three days of no contact, he finally texted.

Hello there, I've been busy I hope you are well, baby. I love and miss you.

Danni was livid! She thought he had some nerve to text her after not speaking to her for three days. How could he think everything was going to be okay just because he had said he loved and missed her? She decided if Charles didn't have time for her, then so be it. She would not call or text him. If he wanted to speak to her, he would have to call her. Although she was crying, she was determined to get through it.

The Thanksgiving holiday was coming up and she told Charles she was going home for the week she was out of school. Danni remembered Charles saying he would not be able to go home for Thanksgiving due to his football schedule. She still cried from missing him. Danni wondered if he was seeing someone else. They had never gone so long without contacting each other. She was worried because she loved him.

Danni flew home and arrived in Santa Barbara a week before Thanksgiving. Her mom picked her up from the airport and was excited to spend time with her. Her dad was out of town for a revival where he was the main speaker and would return home the night before Thanksgiving. The entire ride home, her Mom talked about all the things they would do while she was there. Danni didn't pay much attention to what her Mom was saying, because her thoughts were miles away. She was thinking about Charles and the promises they had made to each other.

They arrived at the house, Danni unpacked, and it started to rain. It turned into a tropical storm. Danni sat in front of the large picturesque window thinking about her brother and how old he would be. Her mom walked in and said, "Dannielle, I want to talk to you."

Danni thought, *Oh crap, here we go...* Her mom always called her Dannielle, never Danni.

"Dannielle, you and Charles are spending too much time on the phone. The first month you left, your cell phone bill almost tripled in cost. Your Daddy changed our plan to unlimited text messages and data. It's ridiculous how much you talk and text him. What on God's green Earth do you two talk about for so long? You two talked at 2:20am for over an hour, and during that time of morning, honey, there's only one thing you two can talk about and that is sin. Dannielle, he is not a good man. God said, if you continue this thing with Charles, he will bring you nothing but misery with a whole lot of pain."

"Mom, you can't pick a man for me; I'm a grown woman." Danni's phone chimed, letting her know she had an incoming text message. She looked at it and it was from Charles.

Mom shook her head and said, "Dannielle, please don't keep doing this!"

"Mom, as you already know, I am preaching on Sunday; can you drop this, please?"

"No, Dannielle! I need to help you see this man isn't who he portrays to be."

"Really, Mom? Who is he?"

"He's a male that sees the potential in you. Did you know he hasn't even phoned his mother in three months? Who does that, Dannielle? She called me and asked how you and her son are doing. I have told you, if the man you're involved with isn't good to his momma, he ain't going to be good to you."

Danni's facial expression changed.

"Yeah, I said it," her mother added.

"Mom, Charles and I are having problems right now, but it won't last. We plan on being together forever, and if he asks me to marry him, I'm going to say yes. He is saved and is getting a degree, which will allow him to take good care of us. We are in love."

Mom shook her head. "Lord, help her, please."

"Mom, I am going to marry Charles!" She realized she raised her voice at her mother. Calmer, she said, "Now, I have to go and study, because I am preaching on Sunday. Excuse me while I go to my room, please."

"Little girl, is that how they speak to their mothers in Massachusetts? Where is this behavior coming from? You may be a college student, but you better recognize who you're speaking to. Miss Dannielle, you know I do recognize where this behavior is coming from. Yes, you go study for Sunday, honey. At least studying will keep your mind off Charles and disrespecting me."

Danni walked off quickly, because she was afraid she was going to disrespect her mom again, and she had never done that before. She was so angry at her mother and frustrated with Charles. *How dare she tell me what to do and I'm grown! How am I supposed to study all pissed off?* She laid across the bed and read Charles' text message:

Hi baby. I know you're mad at me for not calling. I have not been able to balance my time between school, football, and my part-time gig very well. Are you home yet? I'm sorry, Danni. I love you. I really want to talk to you. I called you a few times, but my call went to voicemail. I miss and love you. Can you please call me, baby?

Danni was even more upset at the fact he couldn't balance his schedule for them. They talked about this before they left for school and many times while at school.

She responded to his text.

Hey! I am pissed and disappointed. I feel you don't have time for me anymore. We have talked about this already. I am home, getting ready to study, because I'm preaching on Sunday. I will call you in a couple of hours. The thought of having to preach with all she was going through made her want to cancel speaking, but she knew her dad wouldn't allow her to. She started to pray, and asked God to help her get through the tension between her and her mother. She was hurt because of what her mom had said to her. *Why can't she understand?* She was also struggling with the distance between her and Charles. She needed God to direct her on what to speak about.

Danni loved her church; it was the only church she knew. She'd never spoken on a Sunday morning before, however. Her pastor and father, whom she loved and adored very much, called and checked on her several times while away at college. He called her a week prior and said God laid her on his mind and it was time for her to speak while she was at home, so he told her to prepare herself.

"You will speak at the 11:00am service," he had instructed.

She knew there was no arguing with him. Whatever her Dad wanted, she would do. He hadn't complained to her about Charles, and she was happy about that.

While on her fast, she remembered a scripture in the Bible. II Timothy 2:15 said, *Study to show thyself approved unto God, a workman that needeth not to be ashamed, rightly dividing the word of truth.* She would study and be ready for wherever God wanted her to go and say. When she thought about being the speaker for second service, she knew that was the service most people would be at, versus the 7:00am service. She was nervous.

Ashlee was home from school, too, and hung out with Danni. She planned to support Danni when she spoke that upcoming Sunday. Danni tried contacting two of her friends from college, Gail and Yvonne. Gail and Yvonne flew home from school as well for the holiday. They lived in Los Angeles. They had all become very close friends. Danni told them she was speaking on Sunday and they laughed, because they had always teased her about being a preacher. Yvonne once told her she saw God using Danni and how she was going to travel with her, but she wasn't ready to be a Christian. They laughed about it.

Danni wanted to ask her friends to attend, but decided otherwise, because it was Thanksgiving, and they should be at home with their families. She wished Marie lived nearby, so they could hang out. Danni grabbed her Bible and begin to study for Sunday.

She fasted for two days, drinking only water and remaining prayerful. She and Charles had talked several times, arguing back and forth, hanging up on each other. Eventually, they straightened things out. They were back on track.

Chapter Five

As Danni began to speak, she looked around and it was crowded. It looked like every seat in the sanctuary was taken. Her topic was entitled, *It Is So!*

"David was a short man in stature, not your ideal sexy kind of man. He worked as a shepherd over sheep and smelled stank every day. In I Samuel the 16th verse, God rejected Saul as king over Israel. God chose one of Jesse's sons to be king. Fast forward—Samuel did as God said and took a cow and held a sacrifice unto the Lord and invited Jesse and his sons. You are to anoint the one for me as I indicate. When Samuel saw Jesse's son, Eliab, he thought, *Oh yeah, the Lord's anointed one, tall and very handsome.* You ladies know how when we see a good-looking man, we try to holla at him."

Some of the women in the audience agreed while applauding. Some of the men laughed.

"But in the Word of God, He said, *Do not consider his appearance or his height, for I have rejected him.* God doesn't look at the things people look at, like height, size, and shape, how fine one is... See where I am headed? God

31

looks at the heart. Then, Jesse called for his son, Abinadab, but Samuel said, *The Lord has not chosen this one either.* Jesse called for his son, Shamma, but Samuel said, *Nor has the Lord chosen this one.* Jesse had seven of his sons to pass before Samuel, but Samuel said to him, *The Lord has not chosen these.* Can you imagine all these men, just as fine as they can be? Probably doctors, lawyers, tax accountants, etc. Samuel asked Jesse, *Are these all the sons you have? Jesse responded, 'Well, there is still the youngest but he is attending to the sheep.'* Samuel said, *'Send for him. We will not sit down until he arrives.'* Jesse sends for David and brought him in. He was glowing with a nice tan and had a fine appearance and some handsome features, but he was just so short! Can you hear David say, *It's not the size of the man it's the size of our God!"*

Many were standing up applauding in agreement to what she had said.

"Just because I am not fine according to your definition doesn't mean I don't have a testimony! Come on here! It doesn't mean I have no quality and it doesn't mean I am not anointed. Isn't that just like us?"

Danni's dad was standing, smiling, and clapping. He knew she was ready to move forward in ministry.

Danni continued, "We want the man or woman that is fine with the nice body, and you know they have no morals or integrity. You don't care about quality; you're thinking of your flesh! Jesus!"

Danni stepped back and clapped on that part. She looked at her Dad and they giggled, because when he delivered a sermon, he did the same move.

"David had five stones to throw at Goliath. Goliath no doubt laughed at David, because he knew David didn't stand a chance. Goliath was probably figuring out how he would kill David; however, it's something about taking ownership of the power of the Holy Spirit!"

Many people at this point were standing up, waving their hands at Danni in agreement. A few people cried out with their hands lifted in praise.

"I personally thought having five stones to throw was wise, because if he threw one and missed Goliath, he would have four more left. If he threw another and missed, he would have three more left and so on. David was smart. He must have Googled Goliath and found out Goliath had four brothers, one rock for each one of them, if needed."

Danni's father high-fived with another minister he was standing next to, because he knew God had given her than revelation about the rocks.

"Preach," he yelled.

The crowd was standing and clapping in thanksgiving to God as they received the word from the Lord. Some were healed, some were delivered. While some were still basking in the presence of God, Danni started singing.

"How great is our God? Sing with me, how great is our God? All will see, how great, how great is our God?"

After such a powerful service, Danni was escorted out of the sanctuary into her father's office. Both of her parents were already waiting for her. Her mom held her tight and told her how proud she was of her. Her dad hugged her as well. He kissed her on the check and told her she had done a great job.

She thanked them. Her father told her she was gifted and there was no going backwards. She must continue to move forward in her preaching and ministry. He told her to continue reading the word of God as it would strengthen and guide her.

Rosie laid her hand on Danni's head and prayed for God to cover her and protect her from the tricks of the enemy to stop her growth in Him.

"Lord, she is a dreamer. God, please show her how her life will be if she marries Charles."

Her father looked up and shook his head.

Danni opened her eyes and interrupted her mother's prayer.

"Really, Mom?" Danni moved away from her.

She saw something different in her daughter's face, so she grabbed her and held her as Danni cried.

"Mom, I need you to please stop talking negative about Charles. I told you I love him."

Her mother whispered, "Talk to God, Dannielle, please. He is no good for you and he has only been a Christian for a short time. Please don't let him bring down what God is building in you."

"Mom, please. Not now, I need to greet the people." She walked out of the room.

"You need to stop, or we really will lose Danni forever to Charles," Bishop scolded Rosie.

Chapter Six

On a very chilly Massachusetts night, Danni was studying at her house on her final test as a senior at Harvard University. There was a loud, unfamiliar noise outside that startled her. Her roommates and best friends had completed their finals and were at a party. She heard the noise again. She didn't know what it was, and she wasn't going outside to find out. She turned the lights off, so she could look out the window without whatever was out there looking back at her. She prayed God would protect her and send whatever was outside away. She heard a knock on the door but couldn't imagine who it would be. She wasn't expecting anyone. Her heart was beating fast. Her phone vibrated and saw it was Charles. She answered and whispered hello. He sounded out of breath and she asked what was wrong with him.

"I am soaking wet and fell over a chair in front of your house," he told her.

She was silent, not quite understanding what he said. He told her to open the door. Danni was still confused and asked him to repeat what he said.

"Baby, open the door, I'm soaking wet out here."

Danni ran through the living room, opened the door, and screamed when she saw him. She was ecstatic to see him. He picked her up and held her for a long time. Although he was soaking wet, they kissed and held on to each other. Danni knew their chemistry was strong; she melted in his arms. She stayed strong, because she wanted him to make love to her. She released him and helped him out his wet clothes. He looked at her with passion in his eyes. He grabbed her again and kissed her, out of need more than desire. She showed him to the extra room to change his clothes. He asked to stay in her room, but she declined.

She sat at the desk in the living room with her head in her hands. Charles asked if anything was wrong.

"I need to study for my last final," she said.

"Okay, finish studying. I will watch TV. I love you."

Danni was very smart. She had studied for the past two weeks and was ready to take the test. There was a loud thunder followed by a crackling sound. The lights blinked off and on. Charles wasn't used to this weather and jumped. She laughed at him, and he couldn't help but join in. The next roll of thunder caused Danni to run and jump into

Charles' arms. This time when the lights went off, they didn't come back on. Danni knew what to do. She held Charles' hand while she went to the cabinet to get candles. After spending seven years in Massachusetts, she was now accustomed to this time of weather and had emergency kits around the house. She lit the candles, which created a romantic scene.

Charles pulled her close and kissed her hungrily. She returned everything he gave her. She heard herself moan. Charles opened her bath robe and removed it. He unbuttoned her pajama top and held her breast in his hands. Danni closed her eyes, let her head fall back, and enjoyed his touch and mouth on her body. This time, Charles stopped himself and told her he loved her too much for them to fail God. They held each other, and she told him she loved him. Charles told her he had loved her since they day they met.

"I know your mother isn't crazy about me, but baby, I am totally in love with you and only you. You are the melody to my heart. I can't give you the things you're used to, but I will work on it until I can give you everything you want. Baby, I don't want to wake up another day without you in my arms. I promised you I would earn my degree and I've earned two bachelors and have my dream job back home. We kept us together until you earned your masters and your Ph.D. in Theology; baby, now it's our turn. We've communicated without speaking to each other and we connect on every level of being, I know in my gut you are the one. Our physical chemistry is electric. Baby, just holding hands with you throws my spirit into a whirlwind. We have been comfortable around each other since day one. You are my best friend. Baby, you are my soulmate and I'm not leaving here until I know you will be my wife."

Danni was crying; she had no idea he'd planed this. He pulled out a little black box with a beautiful pear-shaped, half-carat, diamond-cut engagement ring and asked her to be his wife.

"Yes," she answered through tears. Charles put the ring on her finger, picked her up again, and they kissed several times before she screamed that she was getting married. Danni was so excited she called Ashlee, who was with Yvonne, Gail, and Marie, and told them. Ashlee wasn't happy about the news, but she went along with it.

"We should probably call your parents," Charles said.

Her mood quickly changed. She would tell her parents in the morning. In the meantime, Danni remembered she had to get up early for her final, but she couldn't separate herself from Charles. They fell asleep on the couch. Charles had promised he wouldn't do anything she didn't want to. She kissed him and went to her room.

Danni awoke at 2:30a.m. and felt waves of anxiety about telling her parents she was engaged. She knew she had to tell them. She didn't know how to tell her them other than shooting straight. She got off the couch, went to her room, closed the door, and called home. Her father answered the phone and was worried, because it was so early. She told him she was okay and that she had good news.

"Charles flew here and proposed last night. Dad, I'm getting married."

He was quiet and didn't quite know what to say. She said it again.

"Dad, you there? I'm getting married."

"Yes, honey. I heard you."

Her Father was upset for two reasons. First, because Charles did not ask him for his daughter's hand in marriage, and second, he knew Charles was not the one for her.

"I'm going to pass the phone to your mother."

"Danni, you can't do this."

Danni said, "Mom, this isn't up for discussion. Please be happy for me."

"Let me be clear. I do not support this marriage, nor can I give you my blessing."

"That's fine. I have a test early in the morning. I have to go."

Her mother was beyond angry. The fact that Charles hadn't ask her parents for her hand in marriage or even discuss it with them felt disrespectful.

Rosie told her husband that they needed to pray and ask God to show Danni how the marriage will be destructive.

"If we want to have a relationship with our daughter, we have to allow her to make her decisions. When he hurts her, we will be there for her."

Her mother fell to her knees to pray and began to audibly weep.

Chapter Seven

Danni graduated and returned home. She established her own business, and in her second year of business, she reported over $15 million in profit. She named her business The Wright Investment Firm. She employed twenty-five brokers that kept her firm lucrative. She received and attended preaching engagements throughout California. She was 5'9", 175 pounds, caramel-colored, and had flawless skin with high cheekbones that reflected her Choctaw Indian lineage. Her hair was naturally curly and medium in length.

Her and Charles' wedding was the next day, and Danni was nervous. She should've been happy, but happiness wasn't what she felt. God reminded her of the direction He had planned for her, and God's plan did not included Charles.

Danni cried and phoned her godfather, Bishop Jones. He answered the phone and asked if she was okay.

"God told me not to marry Charles!"

He said, "Baby girl, we prayed and fasted about this, and you said God told you *yes*. You know God's voice. Don't allow what your heart feels to contradict what you are hearing. Get on your knees, listen to God, and let me know by noon what your decision is."

Danni thanked him and hung up the phone. As she continued to cry, she thought about all the people that had flown into town to be at her wedding and all the money they'd spent. She decided to marry Charles Cox.

On December 16, Dannielle and Charles were married in the most elegant ceremony. The colors were chocolate and sage. Danni wore a beautiful, crème-colored Donna Karan one-shoulder gown with beads all along the front of the form. She wore her mother's diamond necklace and tennis bracelet set. Her hair was set in curls and pulled up on one side which showed her beautiful almond-shaped face. There stood Prophetess Dannielle J. Wright, who had never showed off her figure before, but her wedding dress showed her thick and curvaceous body.

Upon Danni's entrance, her godfather pulled her a little, and said, "Come on, baby. This is your time."

Danni looked sad.

"What's wrong?" he asked.

"Poppa, I'm not supposed to marry Charles."

"We prayed about this and you said God confirmed Charles is your husband. You just have cold feet. C'mon now, you have these folks looking at you and waiting for you." He pulled her again, but this time a little harder, which caused Danni to start her long walk down the aisle.

Everyone stood to acknowledge her. Her makeup was flawless; she was gorgeous. She looked at Charles and he wiped his eyes. Her bridesmaids were smiling and crying at the same time. Danni thought, *Lord, if I am making a mistake, please forgive me and bless our marriage.*

Charles cried, and she knew she was very much in love with him.

"Thank you," she quietly said to God.

Charles rushed down to receive his bride too soon. Everyone saw his nervousness and eagerness, which made them laugh. Danni laughed as well.

Bishop Wright said, "He's okay, you all. He's never done this before."

There were more laughs.

Charles hugged Danni, and whispered, "You are so beautiful, baby. I love you."

Danni loved when he called her baby. "I love you, too, baby."

She had always been a beautiful woman, but she had gone all out for her wedding day. When she and

Charles walked a few feet away to light the candle, she lifted her gown. The women in the audience gasped at her rhinestone-studded Christian Louboutin peep-toe shoes. Danni smiled and looked toward the audience. She felt a tad bit guilty for spending almost $15,000 on shoes, but this was her day! She didn't wear a head piece, just a simple strand of diamonds around her head.

Charles whispered, "Baby, you look amazing. I can't wait to make love to you."

Danni smiled, "You're so nasty."

"Yes, just for you."

The wedding party consisted of her best friends, Yvonne, Marie, Gail, Ashlee, and a cute little flower girl named Taylor. Her friends wore chocolate, and the flower girl wore sage. Danni's mom wanted to wear all black but decided against it. She didn't want to destroy her relationship with her only child. Charles had already come between them. She prayed God would help her be cordial to him. She wore a beautiful, two-piece crème suit and looked as elegant as always. Danni turned and looked at her mom and smiled at her. Her mom returned the smile, but Danni knew what was behind her smile.

Charles was extremely handsome. He wore an Ermenegildo Zegna three-piece crème suit with brown shoes. Danni had to exhale when she saw him. She was thinking about their honeymoon. During their relationship, they made sure they didn't get into any compromising positions. They had too much to lose in God.

He had four of his friends as the ushers and his nephew Maurice was the ring bearer. They looked dapper in their crème tuxedos with brown vests and bowties. The church was decorated with imported orchids, Danni's favorite flower. The praise team was singing, the sound permeated the sanctuary with worship.

The ceremony started promptly at 6:00p.m. The atmosphere was peaceful yet exciting. Beautiful off-white orchids draped each chair with baby breath all around it. No arch was used, but Danni insisted on communion. Charles stood by Bishop Jones. Charles was 5'11, 275 pounds, had a perfect haircut, and looked dashingly handsome. He knew he was looking good! Bishop Jones saw the look in Charles' eyes.

"Hold on, son. Just a couple more hours and she will be yours." They all laughed.

At the reception, Mr. & Mrs. Charles Cox were introduced to the guests, and they greeted their many family and friends. They finally had a chance to sit down to eat. Danni was famished. Before Danni could take a bite,

Charles whispered, "Let's go, baby, and start our honeymoon."

"Charles, we can't leave our reception yet. We still have to cut the cake for the pictures."

"Okay, watch this." Charles stood and said, "May I have your attention, please? Thank you all for coming out this evening. You could have chosen to go anywhere else. We appreciate and love you all. On behalf of my wife and myself, please enjoy the reception, but we are outchea!"

The guests laughed.

"Honey, the cake!" Danni scolded him.

"Oh yeah. We are going to cut the cake for pictures' sake, and then we out!"

The guests laughed while Charles kept licking his lips. Danni was so embarrassed. The guests laughed for a while. They knew exactly what Charles was alluding to.

After they cut the cake, Charles grabbed his wife's hand and said, "Let's go, baby!"

As they left, some of the guest made jokes about why they were in such a rush to leave. Danni was a little embarrassed about how Charles handled their departure, but she let it go and thought maybe he was nervous or excited.

Danni said, "Baby, I didn't get a chance to say goodbye to my mother or my friends."

"Baby, call her tomorrow. This is our time." He kissed her cheek.

"I need to make a stop and then we will be on our way to the hotel."

"Where do you need to go on our wedding night?"

"I gotta stop by the homeboy's house for a quick minute."

Danni didn't know what to think. She was quiet as she wondered who or what was more important than starting their honeymoon. Charles drove to the south side of Santa Barbara. They pulled up to a house that Danni didn't recognize.

"I'll be right back."

"Wait, you're leaving me in the car alone in this neighborhood?" Danni immediately prayed for safety. "Help me, Jesus!"

Charles returned after about ten minutes.

"Okay, we are on our way." It took about forty minutes to get to the Four Seasons Resort, the Biltmore of Santa Barbara. When they arrived, the doorman opened the door and Danni stepped out. Charles grabbed her hand as they checked into the honeymoon suite for two days before they would leave for England.

As they stepped into the elevator, Charles said, "Baby, don't be upset with me. I want this night to be perfect." He locked the elevator, so no one would have access to their suite. Danni stood there, nervous, as this was their first night together as husband and wife. Charles felt her nervousness.

"Come here, baby." He pulled her close and kissed her neck.

Danni felt weak and thought she would faint, but Charles held her.

"I love you, Mrs. Cox."

"I love you, too, and I'm going to take a quick shower."

"Oh, no you're not. You are mine now."

"Baby, I just want to shower off everyone's hugs and kisses."

He connected his phone to what he picked up from his friend's house. He played some old school R&B music through the Beats Pill. The pill made the music clear and loud enough to hear in every room in their suite. She thought to herself, *that is what he picked up from his friend.* Charles didn't know she had a few Beats Pills at home.

She turned on the shower water, undressed, and got under the running water. The hot water felt good on her body. Charles got in with her and embraced her from behind. She turned and put her arms around him. He kissed her deeply, and she returned her tongue as they explored each other's mouths. Charles' hands were all over her body. She leaned her head back and enjoyed his touch. He kissed her ears, her neck, and then her breasts. Danni exhaled aloud.

"You like it, baby?" Charles asked.

"Mhmm," she moaned. Danni touched him and kissed his chest. He started to moan. Hearing him moan was turning her on. She rubbed his long arms and they locked hands and eyes.

"I love you, Dannielle."

"I love you, too, baby."

"Come on." He held her hand and led her out of the bathroom into the bedroom. He dried her off slowly, savoring the effect he had on her.

She dried him off and could see he was turned on. After looking at her husband's manhood, she whispered, "Thank you, Jesus."

He gently laid her on the bed and looked at her. "Danni, you are absolutely beautiful."

"Thank you, love. Are you going to stare at me all night?"

"No, not all night. I'm just admiring what is mine."

She reached out to him and he laid on the bed with her. Their mouths met again, but this time, with desperation and aggression. He laid on top of her and their bodies moved on each other until it was almost impossible to catch their breath. Danni reached down to hold him in her hand.

"Oh my goodness, Charles."

"Yes, baby. It's all for you, and I can't wait any longer. I need you."

He spread her legs and they held onto each other until he found her spot. She gasped loudly.

"Yes, baby, you feel so good. Baby, look at me."

She couldn't keep her eyes open. They moaned and writhed together, bodies flopping back and forth. She gave back all that he gave her. They gave each other their bodies until they exploded together.

"Baby, you okay?" he asked after a few minutes of catching their breath.

"Yes, baby."

"Sweetie, I'm sorry if I was rough, but you felt so good. I'm going to make you scream. Our night has just begun. I love you, Danni."

"I love you, too," she barely managed to whisper.

Chapter Eight

A year before the wedding, Danni had purchased a home. Her parents were so proud of her. She was financially stable. Although her parents' home was already large enough, Danni added a floor and had many upgrades completed. She loved her parents and wanted to do something nice for them. She would take care of them for the rest of their lives.

Danni's home was in the beautiful city of Santa Barbara, California. It was 15,000-square feet and had seven bedroom suites, four luxurious bathrooms, and three offices. It was located on Eucalyptus Hill Drive. It featured hardwood floors throughout the house, except for the bedrooms and the family room. A spacious and open kitchen and family room overlooked the backyard replete with a built-in BBQ grill, pool, lap pool, spa with waterfall, basketball court, bowling alley, and recording studio. The estate was over five flat acres and was fully fenced in for privacy. There was a huge living room with silver décor and a zebra-print fad den with a huge fireplace. She owned two white Samoyed dogs from Siberia and two Alaskan

Malamutes. All her dogs were breeding dogs. Danni had a staff of six to maintain her estate, including a security team.

Danni promised Charles after they married, she would take off two years from her speaking engagements. Those two years were up, and Danni felt God tugging at her to resume evangelizing.

She called Marie, who was one of the business managers for Prophetess Dannielle Wright-Cox Ministries and asked for a planning meeting to discuss her pending schedule. That would mean Yvonne, Gail, and Ashlee would all need to be a part of the meeting as well. They were friends as well as business managers.

Danni asked Marie to schedule it for the next Friday, at 2:00p.m., at Bouchon's Restaurant on Victoria Street.

Danni had been friends with these women for a long time and she was looking forward to seeing them. They didn't judge each other, even if they felt one was making a mistake. Once, when Yvonne moved in with her boyfriend, they told her she was wrong, because the Bible speaks against pre-marital sex. It was Yvonne's choice, however. They just prayed for her and kept loving her. Yvonne eventually married him.

Danni had four best friends: Ashlee, Gail, Marie, and Yvonne. Ashlee had grown up with Danni. The other three, she met in college, and they all had been best friends ever since. Ashlee was a renowned thespian, had one daughter, and was married to a famous publisher. Gail remained single by choice and was a successful real estate attorney. Marie was a pediatrician and was married to a successful movie director and had one son. Yvonne was married with four children and, along with her husband, owned an NBA team.

With such busy lives, they got together as much as possible for ministry, fun, vacation, and relaxation. They had been together through college, marriage, childbirth, the good, and even the bad. Having their own lives, they had to sacrifice to be an active part of Prophetess Dannielle Wright-Cox Ministries. They traveled with Danni as much as they could when she evangelized throughout the world. Due to their hectic schedules, at least two of them would accompany her, if not all. Danni loved and appreciated their selflessness and the sacrifices they made for ministry. They knew it was about God and not her.

As usual, Danni arrived on time and was first at the restaurant. Ashlee and Yvonne were always late. Gail and Marie arrived together. They greeted each other and started catching up on each other's lives. Ashlee walked in with Yvonne, and they were fussing at each other. Those two always had something going on. Danni loved her sister friends and was glad they all got along great. They had no pretenses and no insecurities about each other, only love and support.

Yvonne asked Danni how married life was. Danni was quiet. Marie thought something was wrong and asked Danni again how she was enjoying married life. Danni remained quiet, because she didn't have the words to tell her friends she wasn't happy with Charles.

Marie asked Danni more firmly how married life was, Danni tried to speak, but tears rolled down her face.

"That man better not have done anything to hurt you. If he did, it is on. He will be got," Ashlee threatened.

"I never liked him anyways. The only reason I even put up with him was because of you, Danni," Ashlee added. Danni tried to respond but couldn't.

"Danni, what the hell is going on?" Gail asked.

"He doesn't make any effort to build our marriage. He spends most of his free time with his friends. Two weeks ago, we had a late dinner. I could tell he was in a rush to eat, just to say he's going to a friend's house and had the nerve to come home around midnight."

Gail asked Danni if she thought he was cheating, but Danni didn't think so. They had a healthy sex life, but he showed her no passion or no romance.

"His friends are first in his life. I have been with him around his friends, and he is so different around them."

Ashlee didn't understand what Danni meant, so she asked for clarification. Danni further explained that his friends smoked marijuana and drank.

"I don't understand why he is comfortable around them when he doesn't indulge in that lifestyle," Danni added.

"He must be doing something. Why would he continue to be around that lifestyle?" Marie added. "Danni, it was no secret that I did not want you with him, but I supported you."

"I shouldn't have married him," Danni blurted out tearfully.

Her friends were shocked.

Yvonne added, "Danni, it made no sense. Charles had wanted you for years. He has you, and now he's trippin' like this."

Danni agreed with them but reminded them she was praying for her marriage.

Yvonne couldn't understand. "This is where we differ. I will not pray for my husband to treat me with love and respect. I will turn him in for another model."

They all laughed.

Feeling a tad bit better, Danni told them that God heard her prayers. She believed things would get better one way or another. She was ready to discuss her schedule.

Marie started, "You are booked in Chicago for two days, Cincinnati for three days, a revival in Bahamas for a week, a prophetic conference in Florida, and girl, we are going to Jamaica, and—"

Yvonne interrupted to tell Danni to look at all the invitations.

Danni thought to herself, *Charles is a good guy and he has a good heart, but I want more and I want to be first in his life. I want to feel his love. I have repeatedly asked him if he's cheating or drinking, but Charles always says no, and just because his friends are doing it doesn't mean he has indulged.*

Ashlee snapped her fingers. "Danni, are you even listening?" Ashlee's tone startled Danni. She apologized and asked her to repeat what she said.

"Focus, Danni. I've been calling you for at least a minute," she continued Her friends wanted answers about what was going on with Danni's marriage...

Danni wanted to confide in them, but she couldn't, not now. She wanted to continue working on her marriage. She knew if he cheated on her, she would be done with him and the marriage. Danni wanted to resume their meeting regarding her schedule.

"Ashlee, what are the other invitations looking like?" Danni asked.

"Listen, Danni. We are all sister friends and we are very concerned about what is going on with you. We can feel your pain."

"I am waiting on God to fix some areas in my marriage, and I'm not ready to discuss those with anyone yet."

All the girls were getting irritated.

Gail started, "Look. Whatever is going on is Charles, Tanya called me last night and told me her daughter saw Charles at some club downtown with some of his friends."

"Just pray for him. Can we get back to my schedule, please?"

Chapter Nine

Danni and her ministry team landed safely in Chicago. Charles had to work and was unable to make it. There was a gentleman standing by two black Cadillac Escalades with a sign that read, *Prophetess Dannielle Cox Ministries*. Danni recognized Elder Frank Robinson. He was assigned to take care of Danni's ministry team. Ashlee and Gail accompanied Danni with her security and administrative staff. Elder Robinson advised the team of their itinerary during their stay in Chicago. Gail didn't like his attitude and told him she would be the contact person for this trip and would provide him with the itinerary she prepared.

Danni snickered to herself and thought, *Poor Elder Robinson doesn't know what it's like to work with Gail.*

Elder Robinson sarcastically replied to Gail that they were headed downtown Chicago to eat lunch at Joe's Seafood and Steak

"That's gonna be a negative. Prophetess doesn't eat before service. Can we please be taken to the hotel?"

Elder Robinson gladly obliged. He was more than willing to drop them all off at the hotel, especially Gail.

Danni interrupted, "Let's get checked into the hotel, and then you all can go eat."

Gail rolled her eyes.

At the hotel, they finally checked in. Gail and Ashlee had adjoining rooms to Danni's and unpacked all the bags. Before they left, they made sure Danni was comfortable. After they left, Danni closed and locked the door. She walked over to the bed and fell on it, thinking about her marital issues with Charles. She called him, and the call went directly to voicemail; she didn't leave a message. She called her parents to let them know she'd made it safely to Chicago.

They chatted for a little, and before she hung up, her mother said her usual line, "Let God use you despite of what is going on in your life."

"I will, Mom. I love you and Dad."

How did she know something was going on? Danni wondered. Next, she texted Charles to let him know she had made it safe and to call her as soon as possible.

Danni fell asleep and woke up four hours later. She grabbed her phone and checked to see if Charles had texted or called her, but he hadn't. She was hurt and began to cry.

She prayed aloud, "Lord, here I am on assignment to minister to Your people, yet my heart is heavy. How can I speak to the people so broken? How can I stand in front of Your people and encourage them when I can't even encourage myself? How can I minister in this condition? Father, word my mouth tonight as I represent you in Jesus' Name. Amen."

As Danni laid there, she heard the voice of the Lord.

Daughter, be still and know that I am your God. Trust me, for I am with thee. I will never leave you nor forsake you. Danni began to cry.

She went to the bathroom, washed her face, and started reading the Bible. The words seemed to just swirl around on the paper. She couldn't comprehend what she was reading and worried she wouldn't have anything to say to the people of God.

The conference theme was *The Life of a Prophet.* First Lady Jones, Danni's godmother, was hosting the conference. They had met several years ago when Danni preached in Gainesville, Georgia, and they had hit it off very well. Danni made sure that she was always available to her. She was the First Lady of Greater Apostolic Pentecostal Church of Morgan Park, which boasted of over 10,000 members. They had so much in common. They both lost their brothers at an early age, they were pastors' kids, the only child, the only girl in their families, and they both carried the same spiritual gifts.

Danni sat on the side of the bed and started singing, *Just Want You* by Travis Greene.

"Take everything, I don't want it, I don't need it, God. Take everything, I don't want it, I don't need it. I just want You, I just want You, I just want You, I just want You. Take everything, I don't want it, I don't need it, God. Take everything, I don't want it, I don't need it, I just want You, I just want You. Take me, I'm Yours, take me, I'm Yours, I just want You. Take me, I'm Yours, take me I'm Yours, I just want You. So God, take everything, I don't want it, I don't need it, God. Take everything I don't want it, I don't need it, God. I just want You, Lord. I just want You. It doesn't matter what I'm going through, I just want You. You are my Savior. I just want you. You are my keeper, I just want You. Hold me, Jesus. I just want You. Take this from me, I just want you. Take this from me, God. I just want You."

Danni sang until she felt the power of the Holy Spirit. She cried out to God in worship and asked God to forgive her for putting her pain above her assignment.

"Abba, please allow us to experience a worship encounter with You." She transitioned to the next song.

Fill my cup, Lord. I lift You up, Lord. Come and quench this thirsting in my soul. Bread of heaven, feed me 'til I want no more. Fill my cup, fill it up and make me whole. Fill my cup, Lord. I lift it up, Lord. Come and quench this thirsting in my soul. Bread of heaven, feed me 'til I want no more. Fill my cup, fill it up and make me whole.

She transitioned to another song.

I need thee oh, I need thee. Every hour, I need Thee. Oh bless me now, my Savior. I come to Thee. God, I'm crying out to You, I need thee oh, I need thee. Every hour, I need thee. Oh bless me now, my Savior. I come, with my hands lifted up. Oh, I come with my cup lifted up, oh Lord. I come just as I am, just as I am. Fill me up, Jesus. Oh Lord, fill me up until I can't hold anymore. Fill me up, Jesus. I want more of You. Fill me up, Jesus. I want more of you and less of me. Squeeze the oil from me, Jesus. More of Your anointing, Jesus. Speak to me, Jesus. I want to hear what You have to say, Lord. Increase me, Jesus. Increase my capacity for You, Jesus. I want more of You, Jesus, I come to thee."

Danni continued to sing with her hands raised, surrendering her will, her pain, and her being to Christ. She sang under the anointing of the Holy Spirit. Ashlee and Gail returned from lunch and walked into their room and felt the presence of God. They began to worship and intercede for Danni. She was speaking in her heavenly language as God empowered and strengthened her like she knew He would.

Danni's cell phone rang. She thought it was Charles, but after looking at caller ID, she saw it was Yvonne. She answered the phone, and Yvonne told her she was praying for her. Yvonne encouraged her to listen to the voice of God and be free in Him. Danni thanked her and told her she loved her before disconnecting the phone call.

Gail knocked on the adjoining door.

"Come in," Danni told her.

Gail walked in saying, "God is here."

Danni giggled. "I heard you speaking in tongues."

"Yes, girl. I needed that touch before service." Ashlee came in next, her face wet from crying and worshipping. She was also ready for service. Danni's phone rang again. It was Marie. Danni answered.

"Let God have his way tonight. Get out of yourself and let God take the lead," Marie shared. Danni agreed and said she would call her later. Marie reminded Danni to have her administrative team to record the service.

Gail asked Danni what she wanted to speak in. Danni chose a two-piece blue suit. Gail set everything out for Danni, packed her garment bag, and told her to be ready by 6:30. Danni agreed.

The car ride to the church went through downtown Chicago, and it was absolutely beautiful. The city had gorgeous lighting and tall beautiful buildings.

After they arrived at the church, Danni and her team were directed to a room where she could change her clothes and prepare for service. Danni heard the praise team, and Gail knew she wanted to be in the sanctuary during praise and worship.

"Um, please don't enter the sanctuary until the pastor's wife has arrived," asked Elder Robinson.

Gail instantly shot him the look. "Danni is a worshipper and prefers to be in service during praise and worship."

"Well, I will let you know when the first lady arrives, he told Gail in a snarky tone."

"We will be in the service and will see the first lady later." Gail, Ashlee, and Danni walked in the sanctuary.

Danni told Gail to take it easy on Elder Robinson, and they all laughed.

The sanctuary was beautifully decorated in purple and gold. As Danni looked around, she thought there had to be at least 10,000 people there. Usually, people didn't arrive on time for praise and worship. Danni felt a sweet spirit of the Lord in the sanctuary.

First Lady walked into the sanctuary, hugged, and chatted with Danni, apologizing for being late. First Lady went to the platform, greeted the congregants, and introduced the speaker, Prophetess Danni Wright-Cox. Danni stood, mounted the platform, and greeted the people of God. She announced she had brought some of her products, books, DVDs and to stop by her table in the lobby with her staff after service.

She scanned the room and felt them pull on her spirit, but before she spoke, she sang *Jehovah is Your Name,* by Ntokozo Mbambo.

Jehovah is Your Name. Jehovah is Your Name.
Jehovah is Your Name Jehovah is Your Name.
Mighty warrior, great in battle, Jehovah is Your
Name. Mighty Warrior, great in battle, Jehovah is
Your Name. Jehovah is Your Name, Jehovah is Your
Name, Jehovah is Your Name.

Mighty warrior, great in battle, Jehovah is Your Name. Mighty warrior, great in battle, Jehovah is Your Name.

A group of bishops entered the sanctuary. As worship went forth, a very tall bishop walked away from the crowd and joined worship.

As Danni sang, Bishop Jiovanni Puccetti lifted his hands. He was struggling with a few things and needed to connect to God. He surrendered to God by lifting his hands, relinquishing his will to God's presence. As he thought about God being the mighty warrior and great in every battle, tears flowed from his eyes.

Danni exhorted, "God's presence is here. He wants to heal and deliver in this place." Cries were heard all over the room and hands were lifted high. You could hear people cry out "Hallelujah" and "Thank you, Jesus."

"There is a sound that precedes the presence of God. Yes, yes we are almost there…" Bishop Puccetti was so caught up in worship that he missed the bishop's procession. He didn't care, because he was getting what he needed. He needed a breakthrough. As the presence of God rested in the sanctuary, Prophetess Danni began to speak from the heart of God about the life of a prophet.

He sat attentively and later learned her name, Prophetess Dannielle Cox...

He whispered to his adjutants, Minister Bates and Minister Shepard, "She is preaching her face off!" They chuckled. He rose to his feet clapping, standing in agreement with the Word of God. He couldn't remember hearing a woman preach under such prophetic anointing since his wife had died. His wife, Nicoletta Perlita, was an amazing and anointed preacher as well.

"Stop questioning who you are in God," Danni continued. "Even if you don't want the title or the responsibility, you cannot deny who you are. There is a great attack on the prophets in this hour. The enemy wants to shut the mouths of every prophet of God. If there has ever been a time for the prophets to speak out on unrighteousness, sin, and everything that opposes God, the time is now! Don't be surprised by the attacks that are happening to you in this season."

Danni looked over the congregation of powerful men and women. Their pain, stress, and confusion pulled at her spirit.

"Do not be alarmed by things that will try to attack your character, your ministry, and your relationships to discredit who you are. The prophetic voice can give insight, direction, clarity, and warning before destruction. The Bible says in II Chronicles, that the sons of Issachar were men that understood the times and knew what Israel ought to do. The prophets today understand the day of the times, why things are happening, the injustices that are happening, and how everything going on in the nation is God trying to get his people to turn their hearts back to Him."

The people clapped, some stood up.

"Anyone who opens their mouths and exposes the enemy is a threat to the enemy. Anyone who is standing up while a lot of insecure, weak pastors are sitting down is a threat. Your attack will come to shut your mouth! Be encouraged. God is with you; God is obligated to you and you will *not* be stopped. He covers those that work for Him. We are not normal. We do not fit in, and you never will, so please stop trying. The natural side of the prophet wants to fit in and have a normal life. What happens is, the prophet still tries to maintain balance in your life and you will align yourself with people who allow you to let your hair down. You allow yourself to be with those that give your life normalcy. Be careful with that. As a prophet, you must encircle those with kindred spirits. Those who understand who you are will hold you accountable from those moments where you want to be normal, during those times when your flesh is weak, and those moments you don't want to be a prophet any longer. You just want to be you, so you can laugh and play. The enemy is so shrewd. He will allow you to connect with those who don't carry the office of a prophet."

Claps could be heard as well as people shouting, "Amen."

Danni continued, "If you're not careful, you will get yourself caught up with the carnal group, and when it's time to speak on behalf of God, they will turn back around and say, *You can't tell us nothing, because you are just like us!* My God! You all know how we are!"

The crowd was standing, clapping, and receiving from the Lord.

"Sit down, sit down, please. You need to hear this teaching from the Lord. This was not the word I thought I would speak tonight. This is straight from the Holy Ghost! Some of you all won't like what I'm about to say, but the office of a prophet is a very, very, lonely walk. Does it feel good? No! Will you be accepted? No, you won't be accepted! Prophet, be careful who you marry. Lady prophets, he must understand your calling. If not, you will appear controlling, which will cause contention." She stopped for a minute while many were clapping and standing. She had to catch her emotions, because she and Charles were going through so much of what she was preaching about. She knew she shouldn't have married him; he couldn't carry her spiritually.

"The office of a prophet and the gift of prophecy come with a heavy burden. Prophetic folks are sensitive to the supernatural. This is important to understand as it relates to environments and relationships. A prophetic ability to exist in certain environments may seem limited to the spouse. It is because the things they are discerning in the spirit realm may be *off*. The prophet spends hours in prayer and is consistent. A prophetic person's tone and presence is often very strong. When they speak, it's with full weight and with the glory of God. Let that sink in right there. Learn your spouse's gifts!"

She stopped again, because the word hit her hard again. She was ministering to her own situation.

"It will ease any tension from your marriage. If you study the Word of God, you will never have a bunch of people in your circle. You will never have a bunch of friends you can mingle with. Be careful who you allow in your inner circle. Get around those who are surrounded around your purpose!"

Many in the crowd were now standing, some were jumping and clapping, and some were high-fiving each other in agreement.

"Jesus had twelve disciples that rode with Him. They were assigned to Him, to make sure He completed His purpose. They were only connected to Jesus, because purpose had to be fulfilled. Out of the twelve disciples, there were only three that He pulled on who were especially dear to Him. Three! Only three were a part of His inner-circle. I'm about to get in trouble on this one, but most pastors are afraid of prophets. Why? They only want God to speak to them!" Applause broke out at that statement. Danni thought about what she had gone through with other ministries, how some of the male pastors mistreated her because she was a female prophet, and how they wanted to reduce her in ministry because of it. Her hands were raised, and she thanked God for the journey.

A woman was so overtaken by God's presence that the Holy Spirit took control and she danced in the spirit.

Danni asked the audience to wait while she joined the sister for a twenty-second praise break. She danced in the spirit for a short period, and then the church broke out in an undignified praise! Danni started dancing again, more folks in the audience were now dancing, some ran around the church, and some sat with their hands raised.

After service and during the meet and greet, Bishop Puccetti was introduced to the lovely Prophetess Danni Wright-Cox.

"I enjoyed service and your delivery of the Word of God."

"Wow. Thank you." As she thanked him, he attempted to give her his business card.

Gail interrupted and greeted the bishop. She gave Danni's card to him.

"If you're interested in booking Prophetess Cox, please call the business office, and I will be glad to personally assist you."

Bishop Puccetti asked her name, and Gail said, noticeably slow, "Elder Gail Lenox."

He reached to shake her hand, laughed, and said, "Nice to meet you. I'm Bishop—"

"Yes, yes, yes—Bishop Jiovanni Puccetti," she interrupted. "I know exactly who you are, and it is indeed my pleasure to meet you."

They laughed at Gail.

Danni could not believe how bold and so forward Gail was being.

"Bishop Puccetti, it's nice to meet you, sir," Danni said.

"Did you just call me sir?" He was shocked.

"I'm sorry. I didn't mean any disrespect. I am giving honor where honor is due," Danni said.

"No offense taken. It was very nice meeting you, too, Prophetess Danielle Wright-Cox."

Danni was ready to go, but Gail was still staring at Bishop Puccetti and couldn't see Danni. Danni finally grabbed her arm and escorted her away.

"Girl, that man is fine and he's single," Gail said.

"Yes, he was handsome, but really, Gail, could you have been any more obvious? You are being so desperate," Danni said.

They all laughed. Gail told them she might consider marriage if it's with him. They all laughed again. Danni moved through the crowd to greet the people.

Chapter Ten

Bishop Puccetti hadn't dated since his wife passed away. He was a highly-sought-after bachelor. People Magazine had featured him in an article regarding the loss of his wife, single parenting, and how he was handling such a large ministry. Ebony Magazine had featured him as one of the most eligible bachelors and the most prominent bishop in Southern California. He was also the owner of Global Christian Magazine, the largest Christian magazine sold in over thirty countries.

Many women wanted the opportunity to be his wife and first lady of New Life Apostolic Worship Cathedral. They had chased him, propositioned him, and even bought him expensive gifts to get his attention. He refused all advances, gifts, and advised that whomever God would send would be what he desired and what he needed. Until then, he promised God he would remain focused on his assignment in the Kingdom. There had been times where he had to cry out to God during seasons where he was weak, and he often testified how God kept him. He wasn't perfect, yet he was determined to stand for Christ and yield himself to be an example of true holiness.

He resided in Malibu, California, in a huge six-bedroom, eight-bathroom, 18,254 square-foot home. His gorgeous two-story Mediterranean estate was located on idyllic Point Dume. It was gated and private; this home was unparalleled in setting, quality, and design. With custom-glass doors, French oak and limestone floors, and a palette of neutral and natural materials throughout, renowned interior designer, Martyn Lawrence Bullard, had infused the best of indoor and outdoor living. Interior space included a spacious living room, dining room, and multiple offices. It also boasted of an exquisite suite with a sitting area, fireplace, a large deck, and spa-like bathroom with inferred traditional sauna, a gym with deck, a Jacuzzi, and so much more. He had world-class manicured grounds, which had made the cover of Good Housekeeping Magazine twice.

He was nineteen when he married his beautiful Nicoletta Perlita, and she was twenty. He was married for twenty-two years to the love of his life. Their love was envied by many. She adored him and called him *her sweetness*. He was totally in love with her. They were good friends, which also made them a very good team. Together, they exuded love, adoration, and had a considerable amount of passion in their marriage. Although she loved him deeply, he lacked certain values she desired. She loved him enough, however, to teach Jiovanni how to romance her, to be affectionate toward her, and how to love her. He'd learned in depth how to complete her.

Nicoletta Perlita birthed two of Jiovanni's greatest joys, their sons, Jiovanni III and Maximo. She was a proud mother; she loved and raised her sons in the fear of God. She knew they would be successful men as she spent quality time with them, praying, teaching, and coaching them while adoring them. Jiovanni loved his boys and spent as much time as he could, training them to be Christian men and men of distinction.

As they grew up, the boys understood the ups and downs of being pastor's kids (PKs). No matter what they went through, they were always in the eye of the church. They were misjudged, mistaken, and misunderstood. Yet, they knew they were the pride of their parents and were destined for greatness. Jiovanni and Nicoletta worked in ministry and founded New Life Apostolic Worship Cathedral, where over 20,000 people attended. Nicoletta was an awesome teacher and an anointed singer. She was very selfless in ministry and had no problem sharing her husband with thousands of people.

Nicoletta had experienced rapid weight loss and suffered from abdominal pain with constant nausea. Jiovanni accompanied her to medical appointments and the fourth doctor's opinion diagnosed her as the other three doctors did, with stage-four ovarian cancer. She was given a month to live. Jiovanni provided the best medical team to remove the cancerous tumors, but chemotherapy, hormone therapy, and radiation were not options at this stage.

Doctor Allen told them the best they could do for her was to keep her comfortable. Jiovanni couldn't believe what he was hearing. He was angry his wife had cancer and angry with God for allowing it.

Jiovanni had to be strong for his wife and his boys. He felt extremely helpless watching her suffer in so much pain. He was confident when he believed she had more fibroid cysts as to why he insisted on additional medical opinions within two weeks. He asked God to completely heal her from cancer. The doctor suggested an intravenous morphine drip for the constant pain; however, that would mean she would be semi-unconscious. Jiovanni gave the doctor authorization to give her the medication. The doctor also suggested he and the boys talk to her during this time as she may not be able to respond to them, but she was still able to hear. The boys cried while telling their loving and wonderful mom how much they loved her. They would pray and leave the room sad.

One day, as she began to doze off, Jiovanni held her hand and whispered that he loved her more than his own life and that she had been an amazing wife, a wonderful lover, an awesome mother, and best friend. "Sleep, baby; get some rest. I love you so much." Nicoletta squeezed Jiovanni's hand, and he broke down crying uncontrollably.

He was devastated by the news of Nicoletta passing. He wasn't with her when she took her last breath. Jiovanni had just left the hospital within minutes at the insistence of Nicoletta's sister to go home, take a shower, eat, and return. He had not left her side for days. By the time he made it home, he received the phone call that she had passed away. In an instant, he'd become helpless and a single father, all within four weeks of finding out his beautiful wife had cancer.

As Jiovanni prayed, he asked God to just help him breathe and to manage the loss of his wife. She was everything a wife could be to a husband, and so much more! She managed the house, the bills, the kids, and she managed him extremely well.

He mumbled a request to God, to help him and his boys.

Chapter Eleven

Charles woke up at 1:00p.m. He didn't immediately recognize his surroundings. He looked around the room and remembered he was in a hotel. He heard the toilet flush and was afraid to look up, because he now remembered where he was and who he was with. He felt guilty, and the longer he laid in bed, the guiltier he felt.

He heard her say good morning, but he didn't respond. He lay there asking God to forgive him for sleeping with Meghan. He suddenly felt bad about what he'd done. He thought about his wife, grabbed his head, and grappled with shame.

He remembered going out with his boys to a club downtown the previous night, which was where he met Meghan. She was attracted to him as well. She asked him to dance, and he obliged her. She asked his name and if he was married. He told her his name and lied, saying he wasn't married. She told him her name and that she had been married for twenty years. Charles was intoxicated and told her she was sexy. She told him he was sexy as well, and they exchanged phone numbers.

He continued to buy drinks, using cash, and was drunk before the night ended. She told him she was going home and hoped he would call her. He said he would. He kissed her openly and passionately before saying goodbye.

They texted often and eventually transitioned into talking on the phone. A few times Meghan called Charles, but her call immediately went to voicemail. When that occurred, it meant he was at home with his wife. After the calls, he would make an excuse to leave the house, then he would return her call. They started spending more time together.

Meghan had five children with her husband.

One evening, they were talking on the phone. Charles told her he had a confession.

"Don't tell me you're bisexual."

"Hell no, but I am married..."

Meghan was upset he had lied to her and asked about his marriage. She asked him how she would be able to trust him again after lying about something so important. Charles reminded her that she was as married as well. She told him she knew he possibly could be married. The night they were at the club, he had bought drinks with cash. That was a sign of a married person, because most people used credit cards.

Charles told her he loved his wife, but she had changed. He told Meghan his wife was a prominent preacher and a phenomenal gospel singer. Meghan asked who she was, and Charles told her.

"Is it the same Dannielle Wright that owns the Wright Brokerage firm?"

Sadly, Charles asked if she knew her, but she didn't. Meghan explained she didn't know her personally, but had definitely heard of her. She asked Charles if he worked with Dannielle; gloomily, Charles said he didn't.

Meghan laughed and asked how he had captured a preacher and a multi-millionaire. Charles was upset and told her there was nothing funny about his situation and that he was a minister as well. Meghan found his statement to be undoubtedly hysterical, and she continued laughing until he told her to shut up.

"If you are a minister, why are you laid next to me? You're a hypocrite."

This angered Charles. "If you don't shut up, I'm going home. Listen, Danni isn't perfect. In fact, she's a liar, she's lazy, and she doesn't listen to me or give me any attention. All she cared about was herself and God. She spends way too much time traveling, and deep down, I think she's cheating on me."

Charles knew Danni didn't cheat on him, but he had to make Danni look wicked to justify his own sinful and immoral actions. Charles didn't know the truth about her. He wanted to blame everything on her, but it wasn't all her fault.

Meghan deflated his ego when she told him nothing had happened sexually with them during their time together. She asked him if he had any health issues causing erectile dysfunctions. Charles was furious. He explained this was new to him, because he'd never cheated before.

Meghan wanted a real date. "Are you concerned about being seen with me?"

"Of course not," he lied. He explained how his wife had a preaching engagement coming up and would be gone for a week.

"We can spend that time together."

"It's a date then," Meghan agreed.

Charles thought about the issues he and Danni had, and it played on him mentally. That's why he believed he couldn't perform sexually with Meghan. Charles was also in the process of losing his construction business due to many complaints filed against him and also repeated violations charged by the City of Santa Barbara. Meghan laughed and told him she knew what he needed and would have it next time they hooked up. She told him she would text him later and left the hotel room.

Chapter Twelve

Charles planned to attend the conference in Bahamas with Danni; however, he wanted to spend more time with Meghan. He was excited about his mistress. Having Meghan around allowed him to become someone else. She was attractive, kind, and they flirted with each other. It gave him a burst of energy he hadn't felt in ages. He felt wanted by someone new, and Meghan made him feel alive. Although he loved Danni, he wasn't strong enough to deny himself. He planned to start an argument with Danni, so he could walk out on her and not attend the conference.

He walked in the bedroom while Danni was packing for their trip.

"We need to spend more time together," he insisted.

"Okay, we can stay a few days after the conference. They could always extend our stay."

"That's not what I meant. Cancel your engagement, so we can spend time here."

She was shocked. "The conference leaders have been promoting this conference for over six months. Why would I do that to them?"

"Are you saying you won't cancel your engagement for me?"

"Please don't do this. We can stay in Bahamas after the conference. I specifically spoke to you about this engagement before I took it. You agreed."

Danni sat on the bed. Her breathing pattern abruptly changed. She was deeply disturbed.

"You have changed," Charles said.

"How?"

"All you think about is you, your job, your ministry, and I feel abandoned. I don't think I'm attending the conference."

She cried because she didn't know where all this was coming from. She was looking forward to Charles attending her biggest engagement ever.

"Charles, you know how much I love and care about you."

"I know, but I'm not in the mood to be in church for a week."

She cried louder. "What's going on with you?"

"You don't see it, but you are the problem. I don't even know if I want to stay in this marriage. I'm not going to the conference and I'm headed to Josh's house. See you when you get back."

He grabbed his keys from the dresser and walked out of the bedroom. Danni heard him run down the stairs and yelled for him, but he didn't answer. She heard the door close.

She called him, and her call went to voicemail. She tried again, the same thing. She left an emotional voicemail.

"Charles, listen. Just come home and we can talk about it. Our bags are packed, and the driver will take us to the airport in two hours. Please call me."

Her words resonated in her mind. She started crying again. She laid on the bed with her face in her hands. She wondered what happened. There was no way she could preach the conference after her husband dropped that on her. She tried texting him to please call her. He never responded to her by text or phone call. She cried uncontrollably.

Charles felt bad about what he'd said and didn't mean to go that far. He loved her, but he wanted to play a little with Meghan. He vowed he would make it up to

Danni when she returned. He knew, no matter what he did, Danni would always forgive him, because that's what the church had instilled in her.

He enjoyed spending time with Meghan. Having a side chick excited him. She listened to him and made everything about him. He couldn't talk about everything with Danni. Meghan took him to places he and Danni couldn't go because of their Christian lifestyle. Danni would never step foot in a strip club. Meghan drank the same type of alcohol Charles liked, and they enjoyed spending moments, sometimes hours, together. Although Charles knew he was wrong, his desire to be with Meghan outweighed his relationship with Christ and his wife.

He knew Danni's flight left at 9:40p.m. and felt bad for setting up the argument and lying to her to be with Meghan. He also knew this trip was the biggest preaching engagement she'd ever been invited to, and that is why he wanted to accompany her. He thought about all the big-time preachers that would be in attendance. He listened to his voicemail and heard Danni's cries and pleas. He didn't respond.

Instead of going to Josh's house, he checked into a hotel outside of Santa Barbara. He wanted to take Meghan out to dinner without worrying about someone seeing them.

He made himself a second drink, but much stronger this time. Meghan knocked on the door of the suite, and Charles greeted her in a silk robe his wife had purchased for him. He had nothing on underneath. He was already tipsy. He reached for her and sloppily kissed her.

"Hold on, Charles. Let me get inside good, first."

"Come on in and make me another drink while I take a piss."

She was disgusted. She made him a drink and crushed two blue pills until they were powdered and slipped them in his drink. She poured more alcohol to cover the powdery taste.

"Hey, baby," he sang after returning from the bathroom.

"You're already sloppy drunk."

"No, I'm not. I'm just excited about spending time with you." Charles kissed her.

"Wait, because I want to take a shower and give you enough time for the pills to kick in."

She wasn't going to risk him thinking about his wife and not being able to perform tonight.

After she showered, Meghan walked in the bedroom with a towel on and found Charles rubbing his manhood.

"This is all for you, baby," Charles bragged.

"Oh yeah," Meghan said, teasing his shaft.

"Yeah, baby," Charles said. He was confused and thought his throbbing hard on was because he was drunk. He couldn't remember ever being affected by Ciroc before, but he swore he'd only had Ciroc with pineapple juice. He felt like the king of the jungle!

Meghan sat on the bed and kissed Charles. He immediately slammed her on her stomach and laid on her.

"I'm going to make you scream." Meghan tried to get Charles to calm down.

"Baby, we got all night."

"Shut up," he shot back. "This is what you came for, since your husband doesn't satisfy you."

By now, Charles was fully drunk. "You know it hurts so good."

She pleaded for him to stop. He continued his savage sex with her. She cried out and tried to get from under his grip, but Charles was too far gone. Meghan knew the effect the pills had on him made it worse. She yelled at him, but he didn't hear her. He only cared about satisfying himself. After almost an hour of sexually abusing Meghan, he slumped on his back. She jumped up, cursed him out, and slapped him.

He didn't understand he had hurt her. He thought he was teasing her the way she liked it.

"Listen, I don't know what you do with your wife, but you need to slow down and make love to me, and not just screw me."

"I'm sorry, baby. Let's try again." Charles apologized and wanted to try it again. This time, Meghan wanted to control their session. She laid Charles on his back and sat on him. As his penis penetrated her, she began to moan. He held her hips to pump more of him inside her until she exploded. Unfortunately, he couldn't.

Breathing hard, Charles told her he couldn't explode. She was okay with it, because by that point, she was exhausted. Charles got up and made another drink and was ready to have sex again, but Meghan wasn't having it.

"I'm done, Charles. You are on your own." She rolled over and tucked the blankets tight around her, so Charles couldn't try to have sex with her again.

Charles laid there with an erection. He didn't understand what was going on. He knew he needed sex and looked at Meghan, but she was already asleep. He thought about his wife and how she must've felt. He suddenly felt a wave of guilt. As he thought about how much he loved Danni, he started to cry. He wished he was with his wife, because she knew how to satisfy him sexually. Sex with Danni was hot and exciting. She was so sexy. He didn't understand why he cheated.

He closed his eyes, whispered, and prayed for God to help him out of the situation, and to forgive his sins. He pleaded for God to help Danni as she preached during the conference. He realized he hurt Danni and didn't know if she would get over what he had done to her.

Hours later, Charles begged God for his erection to go down. Finally, two hours later, the pills started to wear off. He finally fell asleep.

Meghan woke up hungry and nudged Charles.

He was exhausted. "It's too early, and I have a headache."

"Charles, I am hungry. Let's go eat. Hey, do you feel guilty?" Meghan asked.

Charles was trying to go back to sleep, but Meghan would not let him.

"Charles, wake up!"

"Baby, what do you want?"

"Do you feel guilty?"

"About what?"

"Cheating on your wife!"

"Yes," Charles answered.

"Well, I feel guilty, too, but I am not going to stop seeing you. I am falling in love with you, Charles. Do you hear me?"

Charles still had his eyes closed, wanting Meghan to be quiet and go back to sleep.

"Huh?" he grunted.

"I am falling in love with you. Do you love me?"

"Yeah, baby, I do, but right now I need some sleep."

"When is your wife returning?"

"Why?"

"Because, I'm hungry and I want to go out to eat. No more room service."

Charles tried to sit up, but he had a hangover and nausea took over. He rushed to the bathroom to release what he'd ingested the night before. He remembered he went through two bottles of pineapple Ciroc. He also remembered having a hard-on for hours and the pain he felt. He remembered they had amazing sex all night and through the morning, or so he thought... He brushed his teeth and returned to bed.

He reached on the floor and took his phone out his pants, turned it on, and saw six missed calls and nine text messages from his wife. He felt bad, because he knew he should've been with her. He had abandoned his wife. He knew he had hurt Danni this time. He didn't know why he hurt her; he loved her and he loved God. Something had happened inside him. This was all his fault, not Danni's.

"Hey there, are you thinking about your lazy, cheating wife?"

"Hey, hey, don't say that," Charles clapped back.

Meghan was offended. "Well, you said she's lazy, she's a liar, and she's sleeping around in the church, right? You said she's a hypocrite, Charles; isn't that what you told me?"

Charles knew he lied about Danni, but he had to keep up his lies to Meghan, his sidepiece. His silence started to upset her.

"Charles!" she screamed.

"What?! Damn."

"Don't yell at me because you feel guilty. I don't know who the hell you think you're yelling at. I don't need this crap from you."

"Baby, just stop! I'm sorry. Calm down. You get pissed too quick. Calm down," Charles said, trying to soothe her.

Charles propped his head on the pillow and rested quietly. Meghan looked at him and knew he was thinking about his wife again.

Meghan knew she had to get his mind off his wife, so she laid her head on his thigh. She started kissing his thighs, stroking his legs, and he started to get aroused.

"Does your wife do this?" She took his shaft into her mouth, and the thoughts of his wife began to fade.

Chapter Thirteen

Danni preached the conference and stayed an extra three days before she returned home. She arrived home at 11:30 p.m., and Charles wasn't there. The emptiness she felt was overwhelming. She believed he was cheating on her. She opened the refrigerator and saw several bottles of alcohol. Danni emptied each bottle of liquor down the kitchen sink and began to cry. It hurt her. As she cried, she thought about how she always supported him and willingly provided for him financially while he'd been unemployed. She'd covered for him to her parents and the church when she knew he was living foul. When his family wasn't there, she had always been there. Danni always knew they would be together until death separated them or Christ returned. She asked God to expose whatever he was doing and give her the strength she needed to handle it. She eventually cried herself to sleep.

There was a loud noise in the house and it woke Danni. As she looked around, she saw Charles. He was stumbling, trying to make it in the room. She sat up in the bed, and he noticed her watching him.

98

He was slurring, and said, "Hey, beautiful; where you been?"

"Really, Charles? You know exactly where I've been!"

Sarcastically, he said, "Yeah, you were preaching somewhere, huh?

"What is going on with you? Where is this coming from? If you want to be with someone else then go, but don't play with me, Charles."

Charles stumbled into the bathroom and turned the shower on.

She followed him and asked, "Do you realize its 4:30?"

"I'm a grown ass man; I do whatever I want to do. I am sick of you, Danni. All you care about is your job and your ministry. Hell, what about me?" He took a deep breath to control his emotions. "You don't go anywhere with me. You don't spend any time with me. I don't feel like the man of the house."

"Charles, you feel this way because you lost your business, but I have been here for you. You want me to hang out with your friends, knowing how they live? Why would you want me in that environment? That is not fun for me, and it makes me uncomfortable, because that is not how I live my life. I thought we had the same lifestyle."

Shouting, he said, "Maybe I don't want to live that life anymore."

Danni was shocked by his words.

"I am miserable. I can't be the man of the house, because this is your house. You made sure you bought this before we were married." He was trembling. "By the way, I been going to the clubs, and I bet you're too good for that, huh? Why didn't you call me when you were gone?"

Danni tried to hold back her tears. She didn't understand how he could speak to her so indifferently.

"Charles, I texted and phoned you several times, but you didn't answer, nor did you return any of my calls or text messages. What have you been doing that you couldn't contact me, or should I say who were you doing?"

"I ain't been with nobody else, and I am not a kid, so don't question me. And quit crying. I ain't trying to see that!"

Danni burst into tears and left the bathroom. Charles had never disrespected her before. The hurt in her heart was unbearable. He didn't hug her or have an excuse for not calling her. He just treated her badly.

She asked God what was going on with Charles and to expose what he was doing. *He doesn't love me anymore and he rarely comes home after work. He said this is my fault.* She cried herself to sleep.

Charles woke her up by kissing her cheeks, forehead, and then her lips. As he started getting aroused, he said, "I love you, Danni." He kissed her neck and then her breasts. He slid down past her stomach and landed in the place he knew very well; the place she loved for him to be. A strange thought that Charles should wear protection entered her mind. She believed he'd been with another woman. The thought was strong enough for her to stop him from satisfying her body.

"Danni, baby, what's wrong?"

"Charles, you should wear protection."

"What! Why? Girl, we married; just hush and enjoy."

"Have you been with another woman, Charles? And don't lie to me. If we make love, you could jeopardize my life."

"I haven't slept with anyone, now lay down and be quiet."

Danni didn't believe him, but she wanted him so bad. She gave in to him and he made love to her with his tongue first. He loved hearing her moan. Danni closed her eyes, opened her legs wide, and gave herself to her husband.

Danni pulled him up, and they kissed passionately while he stroked her breasts. She reached down to caress him until he spread her legs again and entered her with deep desperation.

He whispered, "Danni, I love you and I'm sorry. baby. You feel so good. I love being inside of you, baby. You love me?"

Moaning and breathing hard, she replied, "Yes, Charles I love you. You feel so good."

Danni couldn't shake the feeling that he should be wearing protection. She pulled him closer and deeper inside her. Charles started breathing hard and yelled, "Baby, explode with me. Oh my God!"

As they made love harder and faster, they both exploded together. As their breathing returned to normal, they held each other. Charles looked at her and said, "Danni, you are so beautiful. Girl, you turn me on!"

"As I should, right? We are so good together. I love you, Mr. Cox."

"I love you, Mrs. Cox."

Charles fell asleep. Danni looked at him and felt better about their marriage. She knew he loved her, and it had to have been the alcohol causing him to speak to her disrespectfully. She fell asleep with her arms around him.

Danni's alarm woke her up at 11:00a.m., and Charles was already up. She texted her secretary to advise her that she would be in the office by 1:00. She showered, brushed her teeth, and was dressed in an hour. As she walked downstairs, she heard Charles on the phone telling someone he missed them.

"Charles," she called out loudly.

"Yes?" He whispered on the phone and ended the call.

Her heart was beating fast and she felt anxious. She couldn't believe that after their night, he was talking to a woman. "Who were you on the phone with?

"Tony, why?"

"When did you start telling Tony you miss him?"

"You always have to start something, Danni. You know that? I have a job interview shortly."

"I know what I heard you say, Charles. Who were you really talking to?" She wanted him to admit he was speaking to a woman.

"I said Tony, so let it go!"

"Charles, what is going on with you? What are you up to?"

"Look, Danni, I'm going through a lot of things right now."

"Like what?" she raised her voice and said, "Talk to me!"

He yelled at her. "I'm not ready to talk about it right now. I might when you get home from work."

"I hope so."

"All right, Danni. I'm gone." Charles walked out the house.

Chapter Fourteen

Danni arrived home from a very busy and draining day at the office, but Charles wasn't home. She showered, changed clothes, and started dinner. She called Charles; he didn't pick up. She texted him and didn't receive a response. Danni was very angry at Charles. She felt like she was going to lose herself emotionally. How dare he treat her like this?

Danni was distraught about her marriage and couldn't eat, so she cleaned the kitchen. She then went to her room, grabbed her Bible, and read until she fell asleep. She slept light, and eventually she felt Charles get into bed. She didn't acknowledge him, nor did he say anything to her. After Danni fell asleep again, she had a dream. In the dream, she saw Charles kissing and holding another woman. The woman had her arms around him and they were kissing very passionately while he caressed her butt. Danni awoke in shock and yelled, "No!" Her heart was racing, her body was tense. She jumped out of bed and woke Charles.

He yelled at her. "What?"

Hysterical, Danni said, "I had a dream and God showed me you're having an affair." Danni choked on her words. Charles knew how God revealed things to Danni in dreams. It caught him off guard.

A few seconds passed, and Charles said, "I never kissed her or had sex with her." He saw the look on Danni's face and he knew she didn't believe him. He got out of bed and sat on the edge of it.

Danni spewed, "You idiot! You just admitted what exactly you've been doing. Oh, my God!" Danni started to feel the pain of what God revealed to her. She felt sick to her stomach and ran into the bathroom to vomit. Charles didn't check on her. As she brushed her teeth, the realization of how the man she loved and married six years ago had devastated her life. She returned to the bedroom and Charles was still sitting on the bed.

He softly said, "Danni, I didn't have sex with her, and please stop crying!"

Unable to halt her sobs, she responded, "How can you do this to me and to us? How long has this been going on? Are you in love with her? I want to know everything. How could you betray me like this?"

Softly, he said, "No, I'm not in love with her and I didn't have sex with her."

Danni looked outside the bedroom window and cried again.

"Charles, how could you? So, this is why you were always gone? You said you've been hanging out with your friends. You are such a liar!"

He didn't answer but continued to look at her. He was very nervous, considering he didn't know how this was going to turn out. Charles thought about how if Danni didn't forgive him, his lifestyle would be in jeopardy.

God had exposed Charles, and because of it, he was not feeling well. He got up and went to the bathroom. He didn't mean for her to find out. He was going to end it. He was at a loss for what to say to her. He knew she was devastated, but he didn't know how to console her.

Charles had the nerve to be upset with God. He had never been affectionate or compassionate, so he had no idea what to do or how to talk to his wife.

He washed his hands and returned to the room. "I want to work things out."

"Yeah right, Charles, of course you do." He knew she was pissed.

Danni sat on the chaise in their bedroom and looked at the clock on her nightstand, it read 3:40a.m. She remembered she was preaching at the 8:00a.m. service at the Remnant Family Worship Center. She immediately grabbed her phone.

Charles asked, "Who are you calling?

She didn't answer him.

He looked very nervous.

Danni began to talk, "Bishop Jones, this is Prophetess Dannielle Cox. Something came up and I can't speak this morning. Please give me a call when you receive this message."

Charles immediately said, "Danni, I met her at a club. She's been married a long time, and since we were having problems, I spoke to her about it, thinking maybe there was something she could say to help us." The more Charles spoke, the worse Danni felt.

"As bad as you have mistreated me and abandoned me in this marriage, I have never gone to another man, for any reason. As weak as you are, I have not gone to another man to talk about our private life. I've done nothing to disrespect our marriage, and I've never cheated on you. At no given time have I ever thought of cheating on you, but you do this to me?"

"Weak? Is that what you think of me?" Charles looked puzzled.

"Only a weak man would cheat, lie, and betray me like you have."

"You don't even talk to me, Danni. You don't listen to me. You just don't understand me."

She replied, "You are a liar and don't even try to turn the blame on me. If you stayed home sometimes, maybe you'd get a conversation or two. But no, you choose to be a coward and cheat. You are so wrong for this! There is nothing you can say that will justify why you chose to be a selfish and pathetic man."

She walked into the bathroom, locked the door behind her, sat on the floor, and screamed. She then did what she knew and prayed. "God, please help me. I don't know what to say or do. This really hurts, and I can't even think straight right now. I need You. Why did this happen?" She wailed and didn't care if Charles heard her.

Charles stood at the door and listened to Danni praying and crying. He immediately walked into the bedroom, grabbed his cell phone, and texted Meghan to let her know that Danni found out and they had to stop, for now. He deleted Meghan's contact information and went back to the bathroom door. He tried to enter, but the door was locked.

Danni heard him, but she couldn't move; her body was numb. She didn't want to talk to him. Her heart ached from the pain he'd caused; it even hurt to breathe. She thought about Bishop Jones and his church.

She prayed again, "Father, how can I preach this morning like this? You want me to speak in front of church folk emotionally broken? They will see right through me. Lord, I can't. I'm going to call Bishop again."

She pulled herself up and opened the door. Charles, being the coward he was, walked away quickly and sat on the bed. Danni looked at the clock and saw that it was now 5:15a.m. She phoned Bishop Jones again but got his voicemail. She didn't leave a message this time. She didn't know what to do. Her alarm went off at 6.

Charles and Danni sat without anyone saying a word.

Charles finally said, "You should go ahead and preach this morning, Danni. They need you."

Danni heard the Spirit of the Lord tell her to go. She asked Charles to go with her, but he declined because he wreaked of alcohol and had a hangover.

Danni said, "So, you cheat, you betray me, you lie to me, and now you're too tired to support me because of a hangover?"

"You have to go; they are expecting you." Charles pleaded with her.

"You have a lot of nerve telling me what I need to do! You need to get your life back! When was the last time you attended church?" Danni's thoughts were interrupted when her phone rang.

"Hello?"

"Good morning, Prophetess Danni. How are you girl?" Danni didn't respond. "Danni, are you okay? Hey, are you there?"

"Yes, I'm here, Yvonne."

"I will be there to pick you up at 7:30, okay?"

"Okay, Yvonne. I will see you soon." Danni ended the call.

Danni's phone rang again. This time it was Marie. "Yes, Marie?"

"God said He is massaging your heart right now, and you must bring forth the word this morning. He will put the words your mouth." Marie's voice broke, and she said "Danni, you will get through this. You must put your hurt on hold until after the service. I will be with Yvonne to pick you up. Ashlee and Gail will meet us at the church. Get up, take a shower, and talk to God."

"Okay." Danni ended the call. She stood and felt dizzy. She looked at Charles sternly.

He looked nervous and uncomfortable but held her gaze. He sat straight up in bed and said, "I did not have sex with her, Danni, and I want to save our marriage. I love you."

As tears streamed down her face, she didn't try to respond to him, because she knew he was lying. She fumbled in her closet, looking for something to wear for church. She settled on a black and white, two-piece suit and her black and purple preacher's robe to speak in. She grabbed her purple shoes and packed everything she needed to get through the service. She then turned on the shower, got in, and started praying.

"Father, please forgive me for all my sins, my thoughts, and my ways that are not like You. Please comfort me this morning, Father, and use me as I avail myself to You. Open my heart and ears so I can hear you clearly. Father, I am your daughter; mend what needs to be mended.

"Heal and deliver even 'him'. Save his life and don't let him die in his sins. Abba, I need You now. I am angry, I am hurt, yet I trust You. I ask You to be with me every step of this day and let the people be receptive to

Your word. Let one soul cry out, 'What must I do to be saved?' In Jesus' Name, Amen."

Danni changed in her dressing room. She put her make up on and curled her hair. She wore it short, spiky, and reddish-blonde. She looked in the mirror to make sure her skirt wasn't tight and none of her body was revealed. She looked amazing in her black and white tailored suit, sheer black stockings, and black Christian Louboutin red bottom shoes. She put diamond studs in her ears, a tennis bracelet on one wrist, and a diamond watch on the other. She walked out her dressing room into the main bedroom, and Charles was still sitting on the bed with his phone next to him.

"You look really pretty."

"Did you call her and tell her I'm aware of what is going on with you two?"

"No, I didn't call anyone. Sweetie, I want to work things out with us."

"So, why is your phone on the bed with you?"

"No reason. It's just right here."

Danni grabbed her iPad, garment bag, purse, and went downstairs to wait for Yvonne and Marie.

As Danni walked downstairs, she mumbled, "Work it out, huh? Fight for the marriage, for what? To be lied to, cheated on, and taken for granted? No! He is a grown boy that finds excuses to blame me for his behaviors. He should have been the leader spiritually, financially, and emotionally. He chose to be a coward!"

Chapter Fifteen

Two hours later, Yvonne and Marie arrived promptly at 7:30. Yvonne grabbed Danni's travel bag and purse and escorted Danni to the car. They both knew something was dreadfully wrong, and they'd been interceding in prayer all morning on Danni's behalf. At this moment, they were hurting for her.

When they arrived at the Remnant Family Worship Center, the three women were escorted into an office by a deacon. Gail and Ashlee were already waiting on Danni. Gail assisted Danni in changing into her preacher's robe. Ashlee looked at Danni and began to intercede for her in the spirit. Gail suggested the others pray as well. After they prayed, Gail told Danni her eyes were sad, but added that God had heard her prayers and she must trust Him. Danni broke down in Gail's arms. Marie began to speak in her heavenly language. Danni knew she had to get herself together, so she asked her friends to wait outside the room. They hugged her and left. Danni sat and asked the Lord to remove the scene from her mind, so she could hear Him clearly. She drank some tea, and Gail knocked on the door and told her it was time to deliver the word.

Danni sat on stage during praise and worship. She participated and joined the praise team as they sung, *Fill me up* by Tasha Cobbs. She lifted her hands and began to worship God. She began to feel better.

As worship came to an end, Bishop Bates introduced Prophetess Dannielle Cox. Danni mounted the platform and greeted the people of God. She became awkwardly quiet for a few seconds. She finally told the church that the Lord had changed her message. All she knew was that, for the first time, she was living Luke 12:48: *For unto whomsoever much is given, of him shall be much required!*

"With great power comes great responsibility. This morning, I stand before you with a word from God, and as broken as I feel, it is my responsibility as a prophet and a woman of God to deliver this word to you.

"It doesn't matter where you're at right now. No matter what your current situation, God is right there. He has reached you where you are spiritually, emotionally, and physically. Please, all over the room, if you would help me lift up Jesus. I can't go on without His presence; hallelujah, come on somebody, say hallelujah! This is a season of the supernatural! Those who have been betrayed and lied to, you need a God-encounter. We want to experience You, God."

The musicians played softly. Danni lifted a hand while the other was holding the microphone. A hush came over the room.

Her eyes closed, and tears streamed down her face. She began to sing Benita Washington's version of *You Are My Strength.*

In the fullness of Your grace, in the power of Your name. You lift me up, You lift me up. In the fullness of Your grace, in the power of Your name, we lift You up. Unfailing love, stronger than mountains, deeper than oceans, reaches to me. You are my strength, strength like no other, hope like no other, reaches to me.

In the fullness of Your grace, in the power of Your name, You lift me up, You lift me up. In the fullness of Your grace, in the power of Your name, You lift me up, You lift me up.

The people of God participated in worship; hands were lifted all over the sanctuary as they worshipped their Lord, Jesus Christ. Tears flowed, and Danni continued to sing:

117

*You are my strength, strength like no other, strength
like no other, reaches to me. Hallelujah, He is our
only strength; He is the only one that can lift us.*

Meanwhile, her friends—Gail, Yvonne, Marie, and
Ashlee—prayed for Danni as they knew she was
emotionally devastated. They stood on stage together,
holding hands and praying that God would lift her heart as
souls were touched and delivered through the Word of God.
Ashlee was very concerned and didn't know how Danni
could go forth in so much pain. She kept her eyes on Danni
and interceded in prayer on her behalf.

Danni continued to exhort, and as the musician
continued to play, she sang,

*Unfailing love, stronger than mountains, deeper
than oceans, reaches to me.*

As the music continued to play softly, heavenly
tongues were heard all over the building. Danni was
speaking in tongues before she began to speak to the
congregation again. She told them, "There are many of us
here this morning in pain—pain from church hurts, pain of
losing someone dear to us, pain from betrayal, pain from a
cheating spouse, pain from lies, pain from being used and
abused, pain from him or her leaving you, pain from our
children living for the enemy, pain from some of our

children in prison, pain from friends walking away, pain from a diagnosis from your doctor, pain because of the lack in your life. Please know that God is our strength, strength like no other, and His strength can reach you if you will just ask Him and trust Him. His strength is made perfect in your weakness. Come on and clap your hands and seal your worship right now with an offering of praise. Only if you believe God is your strength, your joy, able to pick you up. Lift our King all over this place. He's worthy to be praised. Where we are weak, HE is strong, Amen."

A spirit of praise fell in the room. Folks started dancing in the spirit, some ran around the church, and some quietly praised God in their seats.

As Danni was lifted in her spirit, she shared how believers must be determined to separate themselves from anyone or anything that is not directly attached or linked to their purpose. "It is too late to play with your purpose. God will send people in your life, not to loan money to or to take your stuff, but to assist you in fulfilling your purpose. Like Joseph, who was sentenced to jail on a sex crime that he didn't commit, there he found his two people to make his dream a reality. He found the baker and the server, but all Joseph had to do was sleep. Don't stop dreaming because you're in a storm! I don't know who I am talking to this morning, but your identity will lead you to your purpose or destiny. It is your identity that you must be concerned about. Who are you? What is your character like?

"The folk you are around don't believe in you, so you water down your identity. When you know who and whose you are, you don't have to manipulate anyone to get stuff! No ma'am and no sir! Your gifts will make room for you. Tell someone sitting on your row that you may not look like much on the outside, but you are a child of God."

She continued to say, "Watered down folk are intimidated because they don't know who they are. You are trying to fit into other folk's circles, drinking, smoking, partying, sexing, sleeping with him and he's not your husband…" She became quiet, but quickly continued her sermon, "or sleeping with her and she is not your wife. You want popularity because you had popularity in the world and because you're the man or the woman in ministry, you straddled the fence. You are outside of God's will, enjoying sin, but walk in church on Sunday morning and Tuesday bible study with a large Bible like you are living holy. What you don't get is that the circle you're hanging out with in the world, when you leave them, they are laughing at you because they know you are fake. They know that saved folk don't behave the way you do. In fact, the world sees you as a joke!

"When the world loses their jobs, they hustle and sell dope to pay their bills. When we, the saints of the Most High God, lose our jobs, we do the same thing. When the world wants to relax and chill out, they go out and buy Cîroc, Hennessey, Patron, Tequila, and beer. Guess what? When some of the saints want to relax and chill, we do the same thing, but we may get a bottle of Stella Rose wine to justify our decision. You even say that Jesus turned water into wine, so why can't we drink it? The world is laughing at us. Don't you know the world is hoping we get it together, so they can have hope in something beyond themselves?" The folks were standing up and clapping in agreement with the truth.

Danni didn't get the opportunity to continue with her sermon because so many people walked to the altar, got on their knees, and prayed for help. Danni had to shift gears and recognized that there was a spirit of deliverance in the house.

She usually didn't pray for so many people individually, but God led her to do so. Danni had Gail, Yvonne, Ashlee, and Marie with her as she ministered to souls. They were assisting her, and she silently thanked

God for the church altar workers and the deacons who were keeping things flowing on the prayer line.

There was a couple that asked Danni to pray for their marriage. The wife burst into tears and told Danni her husband cheated on her, and he didn't understand the hurt he caused. Danni turned and looked at the man. She thought about Charles. The man told Danni he was godly and sorry. He didn't want to lose his wife and family and was willing to do whatever it took to help them through the pain he caused.

Thankfully, the other ministers began to pray for the other people on the altar. Danni ministered to the couple, tears falling from her eyes as she thought about her own situation and the fact that Charles didn't want to do whatever it took. She began to talk to God on behalf of the couple's marriage in her heavenly tongues.

She had them hold hands and told them, "God must be the center of your lives every day. Renew your walk with God. Ask your wife for forgiveness. You both go to God for forgiveness. It takes more than love to make a marriage work. It takes sacrifice, trust, and loyalty. I don't know what occurred in your marriage, but she is devastated. You two get godly counseling from your pastor. Feed each other with love, read the Word of God together, and find time for the two of you. Communicate and listen to each other's needs. Support each other. Make every effort to rejuvenate your love." As Danni prayed for the couple, she again thought about her own marriage.

After service, Danni was exhausted and wanted to go home, take a shower, and sleep for a week. Her friends were in the room and, as usual, they prayed with her after she ministered to the people of God. This time was different. Ashlee grabbed Danni and held her until Danni started to cry. The others joined her and held Danni, so she could cry freely. They prayed for her. Although they knew through discernment that Danni was hurt from betrayal, they prayed for peace.

Marie started singing softly. *"In the fullness of Your grace, in the power of Your name, You lift me up, You lift me up."* She continued to sing softly and moved to another area of the room while the others are prayed for Danni, her marriage, and her husband. They asked God for direction and to continue to order her steps in this ordeal. Danni couldn't speak; she was vulnerable. She was in so much pain that she could barely breathe. And after being used by God so mightily and so powerfully, she didn't want to breathe anymore; it was just too painful. They sat around her on the floor until she was ready to get up.

They assisted Danni in changing her clothes and got her together to meet the pastor and first lady of the church. Her friends remained with her during the meet and greet. Danni smiled and was humbled and grateful for the gifts she received, but she felt empty and was in the worst pain.

Chapter Sixteen

No one spoke a word on the way to Danni's house. When they arrived, Ashlee and Marie got out of the car, got Danni's garment bag, and waited for Danni to get out. She was in no rush to exit the car. She looked at the beautiful house God had blessed her with before she married Charles. The pain she felt was agonizing. They walked into her house. Ashlee put her things away and wanted to stay with Danni, but Danni said no.

Danni thanked Ashlee and Marie for wanting to stay, but she wanted to be alone and get through the rest of the day. She reminded them that she loved and appreciated them and asked for a favor. "Please lock the doors when you leave." She was pooped.

Danni walked away and climbed the stairs. She didn't notice anything out of order and wondered if Charles was still in bed. Danni walked upstairs, slowly opened the bedroom door, and anticipated him being in bed, but he wasn't there. She sat on the bed, put her face in her hands, and cried. She checked her phone and there was a text from him saying he was stepping out for a few hours with

Rashad. Tears began to flow. She went to the bathroom, turned the shower water on, removed her clothes, and stepped in, relishing in the soothing water.

As she bathed, she asked God why Charles didn't love her enough to be faithful. "Why'd he stopped choosing me? He left the house, knowing I had to preach, and should have been here when I returned." She continued crying, and the voice of the Lord spoke Danni.

I had to expose him to you, because he cannot be a part of your greater. I need you to help build My Kingdom. Daughter, I am here; I will never leave you nor forsake you. I showed you his character, his priority, his demons, and his lack of integrity, but you didn't listen to Me; you married him, knowing what I told you. I am here with you as you go through the process. Trust Me.

Danni cried even harder. She now knew the reason Charles chose to hang out on that day. Her marriage to Charles Cox was over. *Ten years wasted*, she thought, yet she still loved him. She stayed in the shower for almost an hour, got out, and dressed for bed. She phoned Charles, but he didn't answer. She texted him that wherever he was and whoever he was with was where he needed to stay. *I don't want this farce of a marriage with you anymore. I prayed for you, but this marriage is over.*

He quickly responded with a short text: *Okay*.

Danni thought, *That's it? No fight? No begging for forgiveness? Just okay? Wow!* She laid down, fell asleep, and woke six hours later.

Danni laid in bed. She felt unattractive, overweight, and unable to keep her husband happy. The pain in her chest was unbearable, and she felt so hopeless and alone. She smelled food and wondered who was in her house. She observed the monitors and saw Ashlee and Marie in the kitchen cooking.

Danni walked downstairs to the kitchen where Ashlee and Marie were hanging out. Marie made sweet tea and was cooking chicken and dumplings for Danni. It was one of Danni's favorite foods.

Ashlee told Danni she should have known they were not leaving her alone and they were with her no matter what. Danni started crying and told them Charles had cheated on her. Marie was confused and asked Danni if she caught him. Danni told them about the dream God gave her. They were angry and wanted to pack her things for a few days and get her away. Danni told them she had asked Charles not to return, and he was okay with it.

Ashlee was shocked. "That's all he said?"

Danni told them that's all he said and began to share the entire dream God had given her about Charles. Marie asked if she confronted him.

"Yes, but a lot of it I can't remember right now. I know I cried a lot. Initially, he appeared to be remorseful, but only because he was exposed. My heart hurts, not just emotionally, but physically. I've never felt anything like this before; I never knew this type of pain ever existed. He didn't just cheat on me, but he wanted to continue his relationship with her. He even told me that she's married, and because she's been married a long time, he spoke to her about helping us with our struggles."

"What struggles?" Marie asked.

"No marriage is perfect, but I thought we were able to work through it. I found out this morning at 1:30a.m. and had to preach at 8:00am. I couldn't reach Bishop Jones to cancel; I knew I wasn't able to get through it. God told me to hold my peace, and I felt so abandoned. I kept rehearsing in my mind what I could've possibly done to make him betray me. I left this morning so broken, and in my numbness, God wrapped His arms around me and He massaged my heart, so I could get through delivering His word. God never left me. How many people were saved and baptized in Jesus' Name this morning?"

128

"There were over 100 souls reclaimed," Marie said, hugging Danni. "You're gonna get through this." What Marie didn't understand was how Danni was able to minister this morning.

Ashlee said, "Chile, it was God."

Danni said, "I didn't know what God wanted me to say. He came through! Now, I need Him to help me through this, too."

Danni ate the chicken and dumplings, and although she started feeling better physically, there was an emptiness and a sharp pain in her heart.

The doorbell rang, and Danni asked who it could be.

"Yvonne had texted and asked about you, so it's probably Yvonne and Gail at the door," Marie said.

Ashlee let them in, and between them, they had three overnight bags, which made them all laugh. They wanted to stay with Danni for a few days. Danni cried and thanked them for staying, because she really didn't know how she was going to get through the night.

Marie reminded them that after sixteen years of marriage, she had gone through the same thing, and the best thing that derived from her pain was finding Jesus Christ. "God helped me heal, and Danni, God will help you, too.

Let God do the healing, because He knows you. You want it right now, but this will take some time. You're going to have good days and some bad days. Remember to stay prayerful, and those days you don't want to pray, pray anyway! Stay in your word, even when the words don't make sense. Keep reading. God will give you what you need."

The women shared their different stories with Danni, and they all said they'd never felt Charles was the one for Danni.

Danni finished eating and thanked Ashlee for cooking. She told them again she loved them, that she was tired, and was going to bed.

The ladies knew their way around Danni's house and made themselves at home. They loved Danni's house, especially the backyard, and decided to take advantage of it. Gail turned the lights on in the pool, which lit up the entire backyard. They sat on the poolside with their feet in the water, talking and praying for their friend; they knew she was in a lot of pain.

Danni couldn't sleep. Her phone kept chirping with text messages and email notifications. She read the text messages and was almost hoping one was from Charles fighting for her, but it wasn't. They were mostly about the service and business information. She turned the light on, grabbed her Bible, and the Lord led her to Ruth. She knew the story very well, but this time, she read it with a different understanding. Naomi was depressed and devastated. One decision that placed her outside of the will of God caused the death of her husband and two sons; the family legacy was gone.

Danni thought, *When you step out of the will of God, you make deadly decisions that cost.* She tried to document the revelation, but she started to cry. She missed Charles; her bed was empty. She could still smell him. She wondered what he was doing. *Is he with his girlfriend? Probably not. It's almost 3:00am. Surely she would be home with her own husband.*

Danni turned her laptop on and checked her Facebook. She went to his page and couldn't pull it up, because he had unfriended her and blocked her. Danni thought his girlfriend did that, because Charles wasn't computer literate. Danni thought, *Less than twenty-four hours ago, I found out my husband was cheating, and he couldn't care less about how I am coping with it.*

Chapter Seventeen

Later that afternoon, Danni phoned Charles to find out when he'd return to the house to pick up his belongings, but he didn't answer. She texted him telling him to pick up his things. He immediately texted back and said his brother would pick them up. Danni showed Yvonne the text. Yvonne called Gail, Marie, and Ashlee. They went outside and together rolled a large trash bin close to the house, packing up all his clothes and throwing them into the trash bin.

Danni told them not to put his things in the trash, because she wanted to give his belongings to him intact, but they didn't listen to her. They got all his shirts, pants, jeans, t-shirts, socks, shoes, and jewelry and put them in the trash bins and trash bags, right where her friends felt his possessions belonged. Together, they pushed the trash bin to the gate, along with several large trash bags, so when Charles' brother, Stanley, came to pick up his things, the bags would be ready for him.

Danni went in the house, walked upstairs to her bedroom, and sat on Charles' side of the bed. She noticed his wedding ring on the nightstand, behind the lamp. Danni picked it up, closed her eyes, laid across the bed, and cried. After she cried for a while, she got up, cleaned herself up, and returned to her friends.

She told Gail she didn't want anyone to know Charles cheated on her, because she was humiliated. "I am a prophet and didn't see it coming. How could he do this to me? He had no respect or empathy for me. Where did I go wrong?"

Yvonne held Danni and told her she may never know the *whys*, but she would get through it. In fact, Yvonne believed that Danni would get to the point where the shame would dissipate, because she did nothing wrong. She had no reason to be ashamed, but he did. He left God and opened himself to the enemy. He chose to stop living for God, and that's when his life started to crumble. It affected those around him, especially Danni, his wife. The enemy was trying to make sure she didn't get the answers she thought she needed to move forward. Danni couldn't see it yet, but this was going to be a testimony to thousands of hurting people. God would help her get through the process and her sister friends were there with her.

Danni told Ashlee about the dream God showed her about Charles' infidelity and showed her who the woman was. Ashlee told her to show them who she was, but Danni decided against it. She knew her friends might contact the woman, and it wasn't necessary to do that. Later on, Danni slipped and told Ashlee, who found her on Facebook. They looked at her page and Marie commented that the woman was married herself. Danni reminded them Charles had told her the woman was married.

"I'm going to contact the husband," Yvonne shouted, but Danni stopped her. Gail didn't understand why Danni didn't tell the woman's husband, because he should know the trifling whore he married. Danni told them he would find out on his own.

"I don't blame her for not staying in her lane. Charles obviously didn't define a lane for her to stay in. I blame him! He's a coward." Danni continued. "I can't believe this happened to me. He was somebody I loved, who told me he loved me, who had never shown the slightest inclination of dishonesty or moral transgression or disloyalty, as far as I knew. Perhaps I didn't pay attention and assumed we were okay. Recently, I've recognized the monster he's seemed to have become. I no longer knew who he truly was or what he might be capable of. He betrayed me in the worst possible way."

"We can get Meghan's husband to whoop Charles," Marie volunteered.

They all laughed, and Danni reminded them that Charles wasn't worth anyone going to jail.

Later that night, Danni was restless and couldn't sleep. She tossed and turned and kept smelling Charles' scent. It was so strong, she thought he was in the room. When she opened her eyes, she realized he wasn't there. She jumped out of bed and stripped it of the sheets and blankets. She put them in the washer and changed the linens and comforter. She opened the windows, so the room could air out. She felt anger toward him for doing this to her, for cheating, for lying, for acting like the last ten years meant nothing to him, for being as heartless, unreasonable, and unfair. She didn't ever want to smell him again!

Danni finally laid down and pulled the covers up to her neck, and just as she drifted to sleep, her phone rang. She looked at the clock. It was 3:50. She thought it was Charles and grabbed the phone. As she looked at the screen, she saw it was her godmother. Danni answered.

Her godmother said, "Daughter, I spoke to your godfather, and he told me everything that's going on with you. He asked me to give you a call, but I didn't want to until God gave me what to say to you, my dear. I know you're in pain right now, but please know that God heard your cries and He understands your tears. You must go through this to resume the journey God ordained for you. You got off track, love, yet God stayed with you. Brother Charles cannot continue to reap the benefits God designed just for you. He was exposed, so he could no longer sabotage your life. His lifestyle right now would affect your reputation *and* your ministry. God cannot allow this to happen. Trust God during this process. I love you, baby. Bishop and I prayed for you this morning. Get some rest and allow God to cradle you in His arms."

Danni thanked her godmother for calling her and told her she loved her, too.

Danni laid in bed and thought about the words spoken to her. She smiled, thanked God for loving her, and finally fell asleep.

Chapter Eighteen

Days turned into weeks, weeks turned into months, and months turned into almost a year with no phone calls or text messages from Charles. There were many times Danni wanted to text him, but she didn't. She wondered if he thought of her, but she would never know. Danni wondered how she could forgive him for all that he had done to her. She had traveled throughout the world preaching and teaching the Word of God.

The scriptures on forgiveness kept ringing in her spirit. She asked God to teach her how to forgive Charles. She wanted to forgive him, so she could be forgiven for her own sins. She asked God to teach her how to forgive Charles and to show her how to destroy the soul tie she had to him. She didn't want to think about him, to care what he was doing, or who he was doing it with. She wanted to be made whole again.

She started to cry because she missed Charles. She allowed her mind and heart to think of him but realized what she missed most about him is what they never had. What a strange thought.

She would wake up with thoughts of him on her mind. She thought about him during the day, and after praying, she thought about him at night. There were many nights her sleep was disturbed with thoughts of him. She would have dreams about him where he was near death, but she couldn't intercede for him.

One night when Danni couldn't sleep, she grabbed her laptop. An old friend had emailed her and told her that one day Charles would contact her in the middle of the night to apologize and ask for prayer. *He will need you to pray for him. The things Charles is involved with are dangerous. When he calls you, prepare yourself to accept his apology and pray for him.* Danni grunted and thought about how she would not pray for him. He stopped choosing her, so he needed to deal with the consequences of it. She wondered if he'd lost any sleep like she had.

She finally turned on music and fell asleep.

Chapter Nineteen

Danni and Yvonne were grocery shopping at Lazy Acres and saw Rashad, a close friend of Charles. He greeted them, hugged Danni, and asked her how she was doing. Danni said she was fine and asked how he was doing. He told Danni she had always been beautiful, a savvy business woman, and then proceeded to say that Charles wasn't doing well.

Yvonne interrupted and greeted Rashad. He called her Vonnie, which she absolutely hated. She told him to call her by her name, but he insisted on calling her Vonnie. He hugged her and said was good seeing her. Yvonne didn't care for Rashad, so she told him she and Danni needed to get going.

"Danni, I know you…Charles said you cheated on him. That's not true, is it?"

Danni exhaled aloud, rolled her eyes, and shot back, "No, Rashad. He is a liar!"

"I believe you. I didn't believe him when he said it. You deserve better, Danni," Rashad said.

"Hmph, apparently it was meant to be. It was good seeing you. Take care."

Rashad hugged Danni again and whispered in her ear again that Charles wasn't doing well. Yvonne interrupted and said reminded Danni that they were leaving. Rashad said goodbye and walked off. Danni was shocked and unable to move.

Yvonne immediately told Danni, "You will not go backwards. Charles isn't worth it. Let's finish shopping."

Yvonne tried talking about the upcoming trip to Japan, but Danni wasn't paying attention to what she was saying. Instead, Danni was thinking about what Rashad had said. She was angry and sad at the same time. They put the groceries in the car and Danni broke down and cried. She envisioned Charles with her. Danni knew the other woman had been around his friends, drinking; the exact thing Charles wanted her to do. Danni remembered the times she drank with Charles to please him, but she was convicted.

As they pulled through the gates at Danni's house, her parents' car was in the driveway. The security team unloaded the groceries while Yvonne and Danni walked into the house.

Danni's parents greeted her and Yvonne and hugged them. They were concerned about Danni because she'd been very quiet. Yvonne could tell that this wasn't a normal visit, so she told Danni she would be in the den. Danni's mom asked how she was doing. Danni told her she was okay.

Danni's father reminded her there was no need to pretend to be strong. "We love you, baby, and we're always here for you. You do know that, right?"

"I know that, and I'm sorry for not returning your phone calls. I saw Rashad, and he told me that Charles was saying I cheated on him, and that's why he's with Meghan."

"Don't identify her with a name. She's the other woman," her father demanded.

"It's not Meghan's fault; it's Charles' fault, Daddy. He's the one that promised to be faithful. He violated me and our vows."

"I'm proud of the way you're handling it." He hugged her tightly.

"I know it hurts to hear about him, but what do you expect? He is a grown boy that finds excuses and constantly blames you for why he caused you so much pain. I know you, baby, you've always been tough on the surface while hurting internally. You are so much like your daddy," her mom chimed in.

They all smiled.

Her mother continued, "The best thing for you to do is forgive him. We both know the man is a selfish, weak coward who can't handle a woman of quality. He went for the weaker woman who wouldn't question his character and accepted what he had to give. Baby, all you have is time on your side, and as you continue to heal, you're going to forgive that man. If the truth be told, I must forgive him, too. Dannielle, you may not want to hear this right now, but God has someone qualified to love you. Don't be like some women and miss out on the right man because you're waiting on your current man to change."

Danni quickly interjected, "I don't want Charles anymore. I am honestly done with him. I have decided to file for divorce."

Her parents were delighted about the news. They weren't sure where she was emotionally about her failed marriage.

Danni was emotional when she told them she had loved him and had trusted him with her life. She didn't understand how he could change so drastically. As she began to cry, her father held his baby girl.

"You are going to get through this and you will help many people learn and understand how to handle this type of hurt. But, you must go through it to share your journey. I know you would love for him to acknowledge what he has done and apologize for it, but will it make you feel any better, baby? The damage is done; you must forgive him. Dannielle, you are beautiful, successful, and powerful in the Gospel. God opened doors for you to teach the Gospel. Baby, you are the most sought-after female speaker in the country. God has someone for you that will—"

Danni interrupted her him and said, "No, Daddy, don't even say it."

"Don't speak against it. Wait on God. Your true husband, a true man of God, is out there, but he couldn't approach you because you were attached to the Cox name. Now, baby, I need to ask, you did have him sign the prenuptial agreement, right?"

She giggled, and said, "Yes, Dad; he signed it."

Her mom was happy with the news. Her parents laughed and made jokes about it. She told them the divorce should be final in a week. Her parents were surprised, because she had just told them that she had decided to file. Her father asked her why she didn't tell them they were divorcing.

"It was something I decided to do months ago."

Her mom asked if Charles asked for financial assistance.

"He did, but never showed up for the settlement hearing, so I was awarded my finances, real estate, business, and my maiden name."

Danni was serious and said she had been praying and asking God to help her to forgive him. She'd read all the scriptures on forgiveness. "Sometimes, I feel that I've forgiven him and other days, I feel so angry. He moved forward in his life with his girlfriend, and I made a commitment to God that I will go through this process the right way according to the Bible. I will not date anyone until I am legally divorced, and even then, I may not be ready."

"It's a process. Forgiving doesn't mean accepting the wrong behavior; it means detaching yourself from the pain, the frustration, and any bitterness buried within you. Forgiveness will break you free from the entire ordeal. If you harbor hatred against Charles, your personal progress is stifled. The enemy made a complete fool of Charles. He is such a coward; he will not acknowledge or apologize for what he has done, but when you have true forgiveness, Dannielle, you won't be resentful or need him to ask you to forgive him. Baby, you must make peace with the fact that he may never reap what he sowed the way you feel he should. True forgiveness is when you can interact with the person who hurt you without feeling uncomfortable. You didn't create this; he did," said her mom.

Danni's dad teased his wife, and said, "Preach, Baby!"

Danni told her parents she didn't want to see him again.

Her dad reminded her that Charles frequented their church. "You're out in the field and don't see him, but, baby, one day, you will. That is when you will know if you've forgiven him."

Danni was upset. "Why would he go to our church, Mom?"

Her mother said, "Baby, as you know, the church is for those that need help, healing, and deliverance. Trust me when I say, he will come to you for prayer one day. He will need you spiritually, and you must be there to pray for him."

Danni rolled her eyes. "There is no way I will pray for him."

"Oh yes, you will. Not to reconcile, but for God to save him and not allow him to die in sin. Dannielle, he still has a soul, and God loves everyone."

"That's the craziest thing you've ever said to me. Why would I pray for him after all he's done?" She grunted. "He better call Daddy. That's his pastor, not me."

Her mom answered softly. "Dannielle, you must throw betrayal away. You continue to replay it repeatedly in your mind. That area in you won't heal unless you leave it to God. Make up your mind today that you won't relive this anymore. Also, true forgiveness means you don't keep sharing it and telling others what he did and how it made you feel."

Danni quickly responded. "I don't talk to anyone other than my sister friends."

"Good, because you don't want to keep him alive in you. When you continue to talk about the same thing repeatedly, it stays alive in your mind and in your heart. Remember, the Word of God says, I believe in Matthew, *Love your enemies, bless them that curse you, do good to them that hate you, and pray for them which despitefully use you and persecute you.* Regain faith in yourself! The first person you must trust is you, Dannielle. Develop a deep, unbreakable bond with yourself. If you can't trust yourself, who can you trust? Envision your life free of this pain, the betrayal, and him. Baby girl, learn how to control your emotions and, most of all, stay on your face in prayer and in the Word of God. That is going to continue to strengthen you. Remind yourself that, as of today, Charles Cox no longer controls you emotionally."

Danni appreciated the words of encouragement, and it all made sense. "I plan to get through this and forgive him. It's time to move forward."

Her dad said, "Now that's my baby girl. Remember this is *not* unto death. And being home will do you some good."

Danni had been ministering and away from home for two months. Even though she was scheduled to fly out the next day to preach in San Diego at Greater St. Luke Cathedral, it was still nice to be close to family.

Her dad said, "I would love for you to speak at the church tomorrow, but since you have to preach in the afternoon, I will give you a break."

She thanked her dad and acknowledged she also missed seeing everyone.

She thanked her parents again for always being there for her and apologized for causing them so much hurt and embarrassment by marrying Charles.

"Mom, you told me he would hurt me and that he was no good, and you know what? I knew it, too, but I loved him. I thought loving him would make him a better man."

As her parents hugged her, they reminded her of how special she was to them.

Chapter Twenty

Bishop Jiovanni Puccetti preached a thought-provoking sermon at his 8:00a.m. worship service and decided to have one of the other elders in the church preach at 11:00a.m. He sat in his office recliner chair while sipping tea. Thinking out loud, he told God the only thing missing in his life was a wife. It'd been six years since his beautiful wife had passed away. He believed he was ready to be married again.

Jiovanni desired a spiritual woman who could discuss passage of scriptures, share her insight, and receive his as well—a woman who allowed him to lead spiritually, financially, and emotionally. He wanted a woman called by God to preach the word who would assist him in leading his congregation to heaven. It would be a plus would be if she could sing with the power of the Holy Spirit. Jiovanni was very meticulous and knew exactly what he wanted. He desired a strong woman that wasn't afraid to speak her mind yet craved his masculinity and romantic attention. He wanted her to be able to preach with power, but also have the grace and tenderness of a soft being that exuded femininity—a woman he could spoil.

As a mentally stable and mature man, he wanted to find the one worth his commitment. He needed a woman who knew her value, her worth, and wouldn't accept anything less. She would love and adore him, and see him at his best without settling for his worst. She would want him to be the man who the Holy Spirit destined him to be and, in return, he would be the man who spoke life into her, eased any insecurities she may have, and showered her with loyalty and consistency.

His cell phone ringing pulled him away from his thoughts. He recognized the phone number and answered the call from Minister Bates. Minister Bates asked if it was okay if he and Minister Shepard came to see him immediately. Jiovanni agreed and they ended the call. Next, Jiovanni phoned his head deacon and let him know he was expecting the two ministers and to send them upstairs to his office.

As they walked in, Bishop stood to greet them and inquired about the urgency and their wellbeing. Minister Bates asked if he remembered a few years ago, while in Chicago, they heard a woman speak by the name of Prophetess Dannielle Cox. Jiovanni remembered her. He thought about their brief conversation after she preached in Chicago. He'd heard and seen her several times as she ministered at different venues the past couple of years, and they were always cordial with each other. He knew there was something very special about her, but that was up to her husband to explore. Bishop asked them why they were asking. Minister Shepard told him that she was in town and preaching that night at St. Luke Cathedral in San Diego under the name of Prophetess Dannielle Wright; she'd gotten a divorce.

Jiovanni didn't respond right away. He smiled as he thought about her.

Minister Bates said, "You don't have anything scheduled for today. Do you want to go to San Diego for a couple of days? We'll be your armor bearers."

Jiovanni just sat there looking at the two ministers. They all laughed.

Jiovanni told them the private jets were already in use, so they'd have to fly commercial.

"Don't worry about it. We already booked flights to leave at 4:45 today. We'll eat lunch before we leave, head do the airport to arrive in time to check into the hotel and attend the evening service. Can you be ready to leave by noon? asked Minister Bates.

They all laughed again.

Jiovanni told them he would pack a few things and be ready to go to San Diego at noon. He smiled and thanked them. "You two know my heart."

They knew Bishop had followed Danni's ministry after hearing her preach in Chicago. Jiovanni knew she was married, and he would never make a move on a married woman. He respected her and his relationship with Christ.

Bishop sat in his chair, smiled, and asked God out loud, "Father, what is this about?" He thought about the day he'd met her. She had on a beautiful white and silver preacher's robe that was feminine and elegant. Her hair was short and spiky, which exuded confidence. When he heard her sing, he felt the presence of the Holy Spirit. He remembered, because that was the first night he got a breakthrough in his own personal worship after the death of his wife. He asked God again, "Why this is happening now?" But, he didn't hear an answer from God. He remembered she preached, and he had shared with Ministers Bates and Minister Shepard that he wanted to meet her. Minister Bates and Minister Shepard made it happen, but she was already committed to another man. Now, she was divorced.

He stood up, walked into his prayer closet, and began to pray. He was ready to see her again.

Chapter Twenty - One

On Sunday, Danni dressed and was on time for church. She enjoyed praise and worship, and when it came to an end, her mother, First Lady Wright, mounted the platform and exhorted about God's greatness. She acknowledged that her daughter, Prophetess Dannielle, was in the service today. The audience applauded. Danni stood and waved at everyone; it felt good being at her home church.

First Lady Wright asked all the visitors to stand and she welcomed them with love. The congregation knew to approach the visitors in their prospective sections, introduce themselves, shake hands, and make them feel welcome.

Danni walked to a woman and shook her hand, welcoming her to the service. The woman said, "I know who you are. You're an amazing woman of God." Danni thanked her.

As Danni returned to her seat, she scanned the room and prayed silently, *Lord, let something be said to cause someone cry out 'What must I do to be saved?'*. She turned to her right and thought her eyes were playing tricks on her, because in her peripheral she saw him, Charles Cox. This was the first time she had seen him since she asked him to leave the house. He didn't attend any of the divorce proceedings, but filed counter-active paperwork, which was fine with her. She couldn't believe it. He was sitting right there in church.

He waved to her, and Danni quickly rolled her eyes and turned her head away from him. So many memories played through her mind. Danni looked toward him again, and he was still looking at her. He waved again, like she didn't see him the first time. She waved back. Danni noticed he didn't look good anymore; he was so thin. He smiled and mouthed something to her, but she was thankful she didn't understand whatever it was that he said. She turned her face from him.

Danni was glad she was flying to San Diego after first service to speak at an evening service. She felt different. She had forgiven Charles for all he had done in their marriage. She looked at him again and he was still looking at her. He smiled at her and she smiled back. She realized she felt no anger, no hurt, and no feelings from the betrayal. This was what forgiveness felt like. She felt good.

Ashlee walked to the front of the church and sat next to Danni, Gail, Yvonne, and Marie. "Guess who is here at church? Y'all are not going to believe it."

Danni told her she had seen him and waved at him.

Ashlee couldn't believe Danni waved at him.

Yvonne and Marie looked at Charles with mean glares. Danni whispered to them and told them she forgave him. She wasn't going to allow what happened to her control her emotionally. And why should she? Their divorce was final, and she was free!

Gail told them she still couldn't stand him. They all laughed quietly.

Marie reminded them that they were picking Danni up at 2:00p.m. She was looking forward to staying in San Diego for a few days of fun and relaxation with her sister friends. "We should stay for a week in San Diego. There is so much to do there. But in the meantime, I'm going to mean-mug Charles' raggedy tail."

Danni told her not to do that and reminded them they were in church. Ashlee noted that he was still staring at Danni. Danni quickly told them to stop looking at him. Mother Wright sat behind them and told them to hush up, but they continued giggling.

Chapter Twenty-Two

Bishop Puccetti, Minister Bates, and Minister Shepard arrived at the San Diego Lindberg Field airport the same time as Danni, Gail, Yvonne, Marie, Ashlee, and her security team. While Danni and her friends walked to the baggage claim, Gail spotted him. She said excitedly, "You guys are not going to believe who is in this airport."

Danni said, "Gail, you always spot famous people, who is it this time, Idris Alba?"

They laughed until they spotted him.

"Sweet Baby Jesus," Ashlee whispered.

Gail said, "That man is just too fine."

"I can't believe y'all," said Danni. "Please don't embarrass me."

They all arrived at baggage claim at the same time. Bishop Puccetti and his accompanying ministers greeted the ladies. Bishop Puccetti looked at Danni and could not break his stare. Danni felt him looking at her and looked his way. They stared at each other.

Yvonne finally said, "Hello, Bishop Puccetti, how are you?"

He didn't hear her, so Minister Bates walked between Bishop and Danni, and said, "Sir, the young lady is speaking to you."

Jiovanni said, "I'm sorry, what did you say?"

"I said hello, how are you?" Gail repeated.

"I'm great," Jiovanni replied. He was mesmerized by Danni and continued to look at her.

Yvonne broke up the awkwardness and introduced everyone.

Danni continued to look at Jiovanni as well, and asked, "Are you preaching in San Diego?"

"No, Prophet, I am here to hear a friend in the Gospel preach this evening."

"That's very nice of you to do that, Bishop Puccetti."

"That is too formal, please call me Jiovanni. Jio, if you let me call you Dannielle."

"Yes, you may. In fact, my friends call me Danni." She noticed how handsome and tall he was. She looked away from him and started to blush. She was hoping one of her friends would bail her out of the awkward moment, but no one said anything.

"Danni," he repeated.

"Yes," she said softly.

Yvonne mumbled under her breath. "Oh no, Danni is not blushing and talking all soft."

They all laughed softly.

"I like the sound of your voice," Jiovanni said. "I will see you in a few hours at St. Luke Cathedral, right?"

Danni was caught off guard. "I'm sorry, what did you say?"

"I flew here to hear you preach tonight. May I pray with you before you leave?"

Danni was speechless. Jio smiled, took her by her arm, and walked into a corner of the baggage claim, holding her hands and discreetly praying. After he finished, he said, "God bless you, Danni. I'm excited to hear you speak this evening."

She was dazed by his presence.

Finally, Marie, Gail, and Yvonne laughed out loud, and Ashlee said, "We have never seen you blush like that, girl. Go 'head, Dan-Dan!"

That rally had the ladies really laughing.

Danni snapped out of it, and said, "It's not funny; he caught me off guard."

They continued to laugh.

Danni knew she was mesmerized by the great Bishop Puccetti. She asked, "Did he say he flew here to hear me preach tonight? Did he really take time from his busy schedule to support me? Is that what he said? Yvonne, you're the only one who is sane around here. Did he say that?"

"Yes ma'am," Yvonne confirmed. She continued, "I believe Bishop, or shall I say, *Jio,* has a thing for you, girl!"

"Get me to the hotel, so I can get my mind right."

They laughed again, and this time Danni joined in.

The security team grabbed the luggage and located the limousine and van waiting to take them to the hotel. The limousine pulled up at the Hotel Del Coronado on Coronado Beach. Gail got them all checked in. As she pushed the elevator button and the door opened, they all spied a familiar face.

"Hey there! Good seeing you ladies again. May I invite you all for lunch?" Jiovanni asked. "There's a nice restaurant right down the hall."

Danni said, "No, thank you, Jio, I don't eat before I preach. But you all please go and enjoy."

"I understand. I will keep you in my prayers. May God use you well tonight."

"Thank you," Danni responded.

Gail remained with Danni while the rest of them accepted lunch with Jio and his traveling companions.

Chapter Twenty-Three

After preaching a powerful and prophetic sermon, Bishop Wright sat in his office to refresh himself. Deacon Mitchell let him know that Bishop Jones was on the way to his office. Bishop acknowledged, and soon Deacon Mitchell knocked on the office door.

"Come in," said Bishop Wright.

"Bishop, there is an unfamiliar brother in the visitor room, but he insists on speaking to you." He read a piece of paper from his pocket. "His name is Charles Cox. He said he's your son-in-law."

"Yes, yes, send him in, and you can leave us alone. I know this young man."

Deacon Mitchell spoke into the headset and gave approval for Charles to be accompanied to Bishop's office. The door opened and Charles walked in.

"Hey there, Bishop. How are you?"

"I'm fine, son." Bishop stood to hug him. "How are you doing?"

"Not so good, Bishop. How is Danni?"

"Have a seat, Charles. What's going on with you, and why haven't I heard from you?"

"I miss her, Bishop. I messed up and I don't know how to fix it. She doesn't answer my phone calls or text messages."

"Charles, what happened to you?"

"Well, when I lost my job, I lost myself. I didn't feel like the man of the house, so I met someone who made me feel like a man. It was wrong, but I'm better now, Bishop. I want Danni back."

"Charles, watch what you say to me. I am Dannielle's father, and although I'm your pastor, I'm still a man!"

"You're right, Bishop Wright, I shouldn't have said that to you."

"Charles, you don't look like yourself, are you okay?"

"I have some health issues, but I'm working on them. I'm also messed up about what I did to Danni. I want my wife back."

"Charles, you should focus on you. Get your life right with God, because your salvation with Jesus Christ should be your priority. You know how easy it is to return to Christ? Are you ready to make the decision today? There are ministers still here, and there is water in the baptismal pool. You can be reclaimed and rebaptized today."

"Do you think I have a chance with Danni?"

"What I think is that you need to do this for you. If you and Danni never reconcile—"

"Don't say that Bishop, I need her back. I can get her back."

"Son, let me finish my statement. If Danni never gives you another opportunity to reconcile with her, your life with Christ is your priority! Don't allow anything or anyone distract you from your walk with God. By the way, she is doing fine."

"You're right, Bishop. I'm going to get myself together. Did you know she's the only one who loved me through all my issues? She loved me when I didn't even love myself." Charles began to cry. "She prayed for me during our marriage. The night God showed her I messed up, I heard her cry to God for me and for our marriage. I hurt her, I hurt her bad, Bishop, and I must make it right. I didn't want it to happen; it just happened. I know she will forgive me, because nothing or no one can come between me and Danni. She will always love me!"

"The divorce is final right?"

"Yes, Bishop, but I know couples right now that were divorced, and they've remarried. I realize I love Danni, and I know she still loves me. We are going to have the same testimony. I messed up big time, and I confess to you, Bishop, I cheated on my wife and continued a relationship with a woman for years. I thought I wanted something else, but I don't. I can hardly sleep. All I think about is how happy we were. I don't even know what happened to me or why I changed, let alone how I got involved with another woman. Will you call her and set up an appointment for us?"

"Charles, I don't think that's a good idea. You two must agree to counseling. I'm not sure that is what Danni wants."

"You're wrong, Bishop. Watch, I will show you." Charles stood to leave and turned back to say, "Thank you, Bishop, for seeing me. Take care and I will see you soon. I will be back with my wife."

Charles walked out of Bishop Wright's office and closed the door. Bishop shook his head. He knew Danni would not agree to see Charles, let alone participate in reconciliation counseling. He thought about calling Danni to tell her about the conversation, but remembered Danni was speaking in San Diego that evening, so he decided to call her later.

Chapter Twenty-Four

Danni laid on the bed in her suite, meditating on the Word of God and her sermon. As she rested on her knees, she began to pray. "Father, please forgive me for my sins. Abba, I love You. You are the Creator of all things, true source of light and wisdom, origin of all that is. Thank You for calling me to the faith, for planting Your word in my heart and delivering me from my sins. Thank You for calling me to teach Your word and share this good news with others.

"I am overwhelmed and honored that You chose me to teach the Gospel. I feel so inadequate to deliver a word of value about You, Your love, Your sacrifices, and Your benefits. Give me confidence in the power of Your Word. Give me clarity in understanding and proclaiming the truth of Your word. Edify Your church through Your word.

"I am unworthy to be given the privilege of thinking deeply about You that the marvelous angels don't comprehend. Be gracious to me, let a ray of Your light penetrate the darkness of my understanding. Give me confidence in Jesus' Name. You are my God, my Savior, my Redeemer, my Protector, my Provider, my Healer and my Leader. Abba, I am available to You, use me as You want. This evening, Father, I am asking You to heal, deliver, and set free. Father, keep me in Your will as I want to see You one day in peace. Be pleased with me, and if there is anything in me that is not like You, please reveal it to me so I can be free from it.

"Now, Daddy Jesus, Bishop Puccetti is here to support me. I don't understand why, but it's very sweet and thoughtful. Bless him for being here. I thank you for all things, in Jesus' Name, amen."

Danni listened for the Holy Spirit to speak to her. As she laid across the bed, she fell asleep.

Meanwhile, at lunch, Ashlee, Yvonne, and Marie couldn't believe how down to earth Bishop Jiovanni was. They bombarded him with questions about his life, his wife who passed away, his children, and his church.

"Since you ladies have interrogated me, may I ask a few questions as well?"

They all laughed. Marie answered. "I don't know, Bishop. I'm not telling any of Danni's secrets!"

Yvonne and Ashlee agreed and laughed.

Ashlee sarcastically and slowly asked, "What do you want to know, Bishop Jio?"

They all laughed again.

"Is Danni still married?" he inquired.

"Which one of us are you asking?" asked Yvonne.

Bishop Puccetti answered. "I will start with you, Ashlee."

"No, Bishop. Danni is no longer married. Thank the Lord."

"Next question is for Marie. Is she seeing anyone right now?"

"Lawd, I can't be telling my girl's business, man!"

They all laughed, even Jiovanni.

"No, she's not seeing anyone right now," Marie said.

"To Yvonne, do you think I have a chance?" Bishop asked.

Giggling, she responded, "A chance for what, Bishop Jiovanni Puccetti?"

The waiter came with their meals and distributed the plates accordingly. Yvonne was glad for the interruption, because she wasn't going to answer that question. She thought he would forget about it. She knew Danni got invitations to date and proposals often, but she wasn't going to tell him that.

Bishop prayed over the food and they began to eat.

Bishop said, "Yvonne, did you think I would let you forget my question?"

"Oh lawd." She giggled nervously. "I was hoping you did. I suggest you take your time with her. She's just getting over something that happened in her marriage."

"So, tell me, do I have to go through all of you to talk to Danni?"

Everyone laughed.

"If you think we're bad, wait until you talk to Gail. She is the mother hen and is overly protective of Danni. She'll want to run a background on you, check your credit score, your financial status…"

They all laughed loudly. They laughed so hard and loud, the other patrons in the restaurant were looking at them. They started clowning around about Danni and the funny things she's said and done. When they were finally able to calm down, they all were quiet as they went back to eating their meals.

Yvonne said, "We are all best friends and want the best for Danni." She told him how they all met in college with the exception of Ashlee, who had grown up with Danni.

"I understand," he said. "Are you taking food back for Danni to eat?"

"No, she doesn't eat before she speaks, remember? But afterward, she can eat a horse."

This made them all chuckle again.

"No, seriously," Marie said. "Danni can literally eat a horse. After she speaks and ministers, she's starving!"

Laughter was heard throughout the restaurant. By this time, many patrons were listening and laughed along with them.

"Perhaps I can get approval from all of you to ask Danni to dinner after service," he said.

They all answered together. "Yes!" They were being silly.

"Great. Do I need to chat with Gail as well?"

"No, she will be okay with you taking Danni to dinner, but that's all you can do with her," Ashlee answered.

"Let's finish up so we will be on time for service," Bishop said.

The ladies returned to their rooms adjoined to Danni's. They could hear Danni in worship and joined her. As always, they prayed with her about the assignment she was on, bringing the Word of God.

Two hours later, while on their way to service, they crossed the Coronado Bridge. Danni enjoyed the beautiful view from the top.

As they arrived at the church, Danni was escorted to a room reserved for her. Her friends helped her change into the most beautiful white and red preacher's robe. She slipped on her red shoes, prayed, and said, "Let's do this, Holy Spirit."

Danni, Yvonne, and Marie entered the sanctuary and sat on the platform while Gail and Ashlee sat behind them. As the host, Pastor Allen, started to speak, he noticed Bishop Puccetti in the audience and announced that there was a celebrity in the audience. The members looked around as the pastor said, "I am honored and blessed to have a man of God in the house that is humble and powerful in ministry. God has blessed him abundantly, and whenever I need him, he always answers my phone calls. My mentor in the Gospel, Bishop Jiovanni Puccetti, is in the house."

The congregation applauded and gave the bishop a standing ovation.

Pastor Allen continued, "Bishop Puccetti, please share my platform with me and have words." Bishop Puccetti's companions escorted him to the platform.

"Thank you, Pastor Allen, for your kind words. I felt welcomed when I walked through the doors because the presence of the Holy Spirit is in this house, oh bless His name! God has been good to me. I'm a survivor, Amen?"

The audience responded with Amen.

Bishop continued, "On my journey, there were days I didn't think I was going to make it. Wait, let me be honest, days I didn't want to make it. Tell your neighbor, 'But God! Hallelujah!' The enemy set out to destroy me mentally and emotionally. Somebody say, 'But God'!"

The audience yelled back, "But God!"

"Yes, the Holy Spirit is here! I need to calm my spirit down, as I am not the speaker for the night. I am here to support Prophetess Wright, a woman in the Gospel. I heard her for the first time a few years ago, and I became a fan of her ministry. I follow her ministry, because she puts a hurtin' on the kingdom of darkness. I'm going to take my seat, but let me tell you, hold on to your seat, because there is going to be a fresh wind from Heaven blowing in this room to heal and deliver those in need. God bless you all."

The audience applauded.

Bishop Puccetti walked to the pulpit area and the pulpit minister sat him next to Danni. He shook Danni's hand, and said, "God bless you."

Pastor Allen read Danni's biography and introduced her to the church. Danni had never been to this church. Nervous, she walked to the platform and, as usual, began singing *I Feel You Moving* by JJ Hairston and Youthful Praise.

After singing the first verse, Danni encouraged the church to sing with her. The music continued to play, and the church was in complete worship. Some were standing with uplifted hands, some were sitting crying softly, and Danni started to speak. "Come on and worship Him. I know you feel His presence. He is moving, feel the fresh wind of the Holy Spirit."

Danni started speaking in her heavenly language. She walked back and forth on the platform while Bishop Puccetti and Pastor Allen both lay prostrate in the presence of God.

Danni cried out, "He's here to do a work in you, let Him in. Let Him heal you right now. Give Him the area of pain that stops you from moving forward, He's here. Father, thank You for being here, a place I've never been before. Speak through me, God, because if You don't, I have nothing to say. We honor You, Abba. We will wait until You say to move. Whatever You want to happen tonight, Father, we move out of Your way for You to heal.

Save Lord. Someone needs to feel Your touch, Your power. Let Your people recognize Your voice and not mine. In Jesus' Name, Amen."

As the music continued to play softly, she continued, "I feel You moving, Abba. God deserves your honor, your praise, and your worship." She lifted her hands to God and said, "God, You deserve it. Thank You, Father, for being in this place. I honor God today and I'm grateful for the angel of this house, Pastor Allen, and his beautiful wife, Lady Mae Allen. I'm grateful for my assistants who work diligently to keep up with my engagements and try to keep me in line. My sister friends have supported me for many, many years. Thank you, Ashlee, Gail, Yvonne, and Marie. Elders, ministers, and people of God, to you, I say, praise the Lord."

The audience echoed her sentiment in response.

"If you will be so kind, please turn with me in your bible to II Corinthians 5:17 and Matthew 15:21-28." Danni read the scriptures. "As we marinate on these passages of scripture, remember that the Canaanite woman came to Jesus because she was experiencing crisis, chaos, and confusion. She had a daughter that had behavior issues. There was chaos, crisis, and confusion.

"This evening, you may have someone or something in your life that is not behaving properly. You may have someone in your life that is mistreating you. You may have someone in your life that has betrayed you. You all may have someone in your life that you love, but they don't love you back. In the scripture, Jesus was on an assignment and was interrupted for a request. Reading this passage, I could tell that the Canaanite woman had a crisis, she had chaos, and she was confused because of how she prayed. Listen to this: *'Have mercy on me, O Lord, thou son of David!'* What she was saying was Lord help me!

"The Canaanite woman was hurting because of her daughter. Her daughter's behavior was uncontrollable because she was possessed by a demon. I can tell this woman was in a desperate state because of the simplicity of her prayer. When you need God *right now*, you don't have time for a long drawn out prayer. When you are in a desperate situation you holler, 'Lord, help me!' Can I get just a few folks that will admit in their darkest hour is when we've learned how to simplify our prayers?"

Some of the members clapped, others responded verbally in agreement.

"Jesus was traveling through the city, preaching the Gospel, and was beckoned by a desperate sista. Notice her prayer request in the scripture, 'Jesus the son of David, have mercy on me' was not about a car. It wasn't about house, nor was it for money, clothes, or Christian Louboutin red bottom shoes. Her prayer is for Jesus to give her mercy. Her child was acting out and she was asking mercy for herself. It implies that the woman may be blaming herself for the condition of her daughter. She was, no doubt, thinking like some mothers do. I'm not a mother yet, so I can't exactly relate. However, she was doubting herself as a mother. 'If I was a better mother, my child wouldn't be cutting up this way.' Some of us think, 'If I was a better wife, my husband would not have cheated' or 'If I was a better employee, I would not have lost my job.' Do you know it doesn't matter how wonderful you are, bad things do happen to good people?"

Some people were standing and clapping in agreement.

"You may be saying, 'It's not my child, but I have someone in my house who is not treating me right, not loyal to me, and not loving me the way God told him to love me. No, no, Prophetess Wright, I am not the reason he did me wrong.' Someone else is saying, 'Prophetess, it is not my child and I live alone, but someone on my job is smiling in my face but doing everything they can to destroy my reputation and my character. They don't understand why I have the position I have without a degree, and they have a Doctorate degree and report to little non-degreed me! They don't understand the favor God has on my life.' Can I get 200 of you that fit into this category to give God some praise?"

The folks were standing and praising God.

"Someone else is saying, 'Prophetess, it's not my husband. It is not even my job, but it is someone who keeps talking bad about me. They talk about my husband and they're even talking about my children. When I dance on top of all this and praise God like I am losing my mind, they say it doesn't take all that. If they knew what I am going through right now and have had to deal with the past few months, then and only then, would they understand why I praise God so hard and why I am so loud in my praise.' Oh, I feel God right now y'all. Hallelujah!"

The people were on their feet applauding.

Bishop Puccetti yelled out, "Work it, preacher!"

Danni continued. "If God has not done anything for you, then I understand why you just sit there looking around. But, if God has moved on your behalf this month, this week, tell your neighbor, 'Move over and give me space to give God praise'."

The audience looked at their neighbor and repeated what Danni said.

"I gotta praise and I gotta get it out! Someone is saying, 'Prophetess, it's not my child, I don't have a husband or a wife, I live alone, and it's not my job. It's me! I don't trust anyone. Women are hateful and mean; the men in my past have mistreated me. I testified about an area where I received deliverance and folk are holding me hostage to it!' Don't you know the greatest enemy in your life is the one you see in the mirror? Men and women of God, it is time to let your past go! If God delivered you from homosexuality, you have a praise. If God delivered you from stealing, you have a praise. If God delivered you from lying, you have a reason to praise Him. If God delivered you from being two-faced, you have a praise. If God delivered you from drugs and alcohol, you better give God a praise! My God!" Danni jumped up and down in the spirit, along with many in the church.

"Thank God for mercy in our lives. Stop the music. I know you all want to dance this evening, but give me a few more minutes and we are all going in together!

"The woman asks God for mercy, which means God is not punishing us for our sins deserved, we are delivered from judgment. Mercy covers some stuff you shouldn't have done. You went to places you had no business going; you slept with someone that didn't belong to you. Mercy! If you can't dance over mercy, you won't understand grace! Grace kept you from contracting a disease he or she had while you were sexing them. My God! Y'all, I'm warning you right now, I feel free in my spirit and I feel a mercy dance right about now.

"What you've been through this year, you should be dead, just from the stress of it. You should have lost your mind. In fact, the pain was so unbearable, you wanted to lose your mind and walk around numb. Tell God, 'The problem is me!' I'm shouting this evening for mercy. It woke me up and grace got me here today. Hallelujah! Mercy put clapping in my hands while grace allowed me to go forth in a dance. You know God should have killed you dead because of what you've done, but His grace and mercy saved you. Abba, help me get through this sermon." Danni's voice and volume escalated out of excitement of sharing the Word of God.

"In the scripture, it says Jesus dissed her. I mean He did not respond with even one word! This woman was in a desperate situation. God was giving everyone else a word, and there she was, in a major situation, but determined to hear from Jesus.

"John 1:1 says, *In the beginning was the word, and the word was with God, and the word was God.* So, how is it, if He is the word, but doesn't have a word for the woman's situation? Someone ask me why did Jesus diss her?"

The audience asked together.

"I'm glad you asked. It's because God wants us to know that He's not moved by our desperation. Oh, you all are quiet now! In your desperation, He didn't give you what you asked for, because if He would have given you everything you asked for, maybe those things would have been good *to* you, but not good *for* you.

"I can make it without money, and I can even make it without a honey, but I can't make it without a word from the Lord! I just need about 500 of you all to know my dance is not for the doors he's opened, it is for the doors He has shut! We need to give God praise for the NO! Who am I preaching to this evening? You should be thanking God for the closed doors. Thank God you didn't marry that man or woman! Thank God you didn't buy that particular house!"

Folks were standing and clapping their hands. Danni noticed Bishop Puccetti on his feet as well. She waited until the crowd quieted down.

181

"In desperation, sometimes you make deadly decisions. There are times when God leaves you in desperate states to teach you how to trust Him. Isaiah 40:31 tells us, *'But they that wait upon the Lord shall renew their strength; they shall mount up with wings as eagles; they shall run and not be weary, they shall walk and not faint.'*

"In our text, the woman didn't go to an adjutant, deacon, security guard, or elder. She went directly to Jesus. The next scripture says she had to deal with disciples saying she was bothering them. The disciples asked Jesus to send her away because she was bothering them. The message version states she was driving them crazy! The disciples lied on her. She asked a singular, 'Jesus, have mercy on me.' Let me give you all a free tip. Your praise is no good until it bothers somebody! You may as well do a row check right now. Ask your neighbor, 'Does my praise bother you? If you thought I danced like a crazy person last week, you ain't seen nothing yet! Today, my praise is going to bother you, because when I think of the goodness of Jesus and everything He has carried me through…"

People were standing and clapping, some jumping up and down in the spirit.

"In the passage, the disciples wanted to send her away, because she didn't know protocol. Oh, but verse 24 says, '*But HE answered, "I am not sent but unto the lost sheep of the house of Israel'!*" Umm, it appears bad for Jesus right now. She's a Canaanite woman, she hasn't attended an Apostolic conference, a Church of God in Christ conference, or a Baptist convention. She's off the street and has no clue what Jesus was talking about.

"Have you ever thought that sometimes the answer God gives you doesn't make sense? You asked for tall man, He sends you a short one; you asked for an athletic build, and God gave you a big, beautiful woman. Sometimes, His answers do not make sense!

"I don't know about you all, but sometimes I have to ask God, 'Did you hear my request, Father? Did you get me confused with someone else?' Sometimes there are things I read in the bible that just don't make sense. Can I share a few with you?"

The audience yelled back a resounding *"Yes!"*

"Okay, here's one. 'Bless them that despitefully use you.' Really? Lord, you want me to bless someone that has purposely used and abused me? What about this one? 'If someone slaps you, don't slap them back.' Huh? He said to turn the other cheek. Wait, another one that messes me up says, 'If someone ask you to go a mile, go an extra mile for them.' I'm tired from the first mile, Lord! 'Give and it shall be given unto you.' I don't have anything to give."

The audience roared with laughter along with Danni.

"Sometimes, the answers won't make sense. The Canaanite woman is off the street, she hasn't been churched, and He gives her a theological dissertation? She was like what in the world? All she knows is she needs help.

"Verse 25 says, 'Then came she and worshipped him saying, Lord help me.' The answer doesn't make sense, but it didn't stop her praise. Even after that theological dissertation, she said, 'You are still holy. I yet love You, Jesus, and You are worthy to be praised. Thank you, anyway.' Does the answer from Abba always have to make sense for you to worship Him?

"Verse 26. 'But He answered and said, "It is not meant to take the children's bread and to cast it to dogs."'" Listen, it wasn't Jesus' response, it was His timing! He answered her *after* worship took place. I expected that answer pre-worship not post-worship, why? Well, I am glad you asked."

There was laughter in the audience.

"Hold on to your seats, because I have the answer. God cannot be manipulated by your worship! Some of us use worship as a magic wand. Some of us believe it can pay for your blessings, some even think they can purchase anointing online, but the devil is a liar!

"I worship Him, not because of what He gives me or how He provides for me, but because of who He is. When I pull on the Holy Spirit through worship, I let Him know how much I love and adore Him. It should cause you to repent, then enjoy His presence. He is looking for real worship! Yes, I know when you attend the worship conference you were told if you say hallelujah fifty times and thank you Jesus twenty-five times that it will move God. No ma'am and no sir. The mere fact that He saved your soul should make you want to put your head back and give Him praise!"

Some of the congregants started to dance. The power of God fell in the church and, not only Danni, but the entire platform including Bishop Puccetti, Pastor Allen, and the ministers were giving God praise through dance.

Danni walked off the platform, accompanied by Ashlee and Yvonne, laying her hands on several people to pray for them. There was a man with his hands lifted. She laid her hand on his forehead and prayed for him. She spoke to his spirit. "Man of God, your name is Malik Taylor?"

He opened his eyes in amazement. "Yes."

Danni asked one of the elders to lay his hand on the man's stomach. Danni laid her hand on the elder's hand and said, "God has healed you of prostate cancer."

Before she could finish, he fell to the floor in the spirit, and the church went into high praise. Several people surrounded the man on the floor.

Danni ask one of the women, "Who is this man to you?"

She said, "He is my husband. He has stage four prostate cancer, and two days ago, he was given six months to live."

Danni said, "This was two days ago?"

Crying, said the woman answered, "Yes ma'am."

Danni held the woman's hand, and said, "Not so! I decree and declare according to the Word of God, he no longer has cancer. Take him back to the doctor and the doctor won't find a trace of cancer in his body. Come back to the church and tell Pastor Allen about the results."

The woman fell in the spirit.

"This is the miracle this church needs to see. God did it! We need to give God praise!" Danni danced, and the church went into another high praise of thanksgiving.

As Danni tried to return to the platform, a man forcefully grabbed her arm. Several men moved quickly toward Danni. She looked up and Bishop Puccetti was already standing in between her and the man.

Danni asked the man, "What do you want from God?" She noticed, although the man was dirty and probably homeless, his skin was flawless. He had a glow on his face.

He said, "I was walking by the church. I heard you singing, so I walked in and stayed in the back. I haven't eaten or showered in days, so I didn't want to sit in the church. Lady, I have AIDS. I had lesions on my face, my arms, my legs, and my hands before I walked through the door. I heard you ask who wants to be healed. I raised my hand in the back, and instantly, I felt something warm in my body. It scared me because I didn't know what it was. I looked at my hands, and the ugly scars were gone. I felt my face, and there was no pain, no sores. I looked in the mirror back there, and my face is completely clear of the lesions. I went to the bathroom, and I no longer have any sores or scars on any parts of my body." He began to cry. "I believe God healed me!"

Danni was so overwhelmed by the healing of God, she started dancing again along with the rest of the church. When she was able to speak, she noticed Bishop Puccetti ministering to the man. There was nothing else she could say. God had taken over the service. She gave the microphone to Pastor Allen.

At her seat, Danni knelt and thanked God for showing up, healing, and delivering His people. Her friends prayed over her as well. Bishop Puccetti walked to where Danni was kneeled down, laid his hand on her, and prayed for God to replenish her strength.

The power of the Holy Spirit was still strong. Danni stood and started dancing again. Bishop Puccetti hugged Pastor Allen and thanked him for the opportunity to share his pulpit. To the church he said, "I am encouraged tonight that no matter what God's answer is, we must trust Him and have faith that God has our backs. Amen! My God! Prophetess didn't have a chance to finish preaching on this passage, but there is something God cannot say no to. It's in the text. Further in the text, He looks at the woman and says, 'Woman your faith is something else!' Ask your neighbor, 'After all that you have gone through in the last year, do you still have your faith?' He said your faith is unbelievable. You still have joy and were able to praise Him! There is a reason you're standing next to someone whose faith is depleted. You have been assigned to speak faith into them. Tell them, 'If I had of gone through what you went through, I would have lost my mind, but thank God for faith!' Come on and prophecy to your neighbor! My God! Lastly, the text says, and you have to get this, 'Her daughter was healed an hour from now.' We need to look at the time, because in an hour, your marriage will be healed, your kids will return to the Lord, and your situation will turn around. Let's celebrate our hour right now!"

He started dancing along with the people of God. After another twenty minutes of dancing, Bishop Puccetti said, "Thank you, Jesus, for Your presence in this house, and thank you, Prophetess Wright, for allowing God to use you to speak to His people."

Danni smiled at him.

"How many of you all are encouraged tonight? I still feel the presence of the Holy Spirit." He broke out in dance again and the church followed him.

After service, Gail and Ashlee stayed with Danni as she shook hundreds of hands. Yvonne and Marie had their hands full at the vending table, selling Danni's DVDs and books.

Gail and Ashlee escorted Danni to her designated room to change her clothes and refresh herself. Gail handed an envelope to Danni.

Danni opened it and said, "It's from Bishop Puccetti."

"Oh no, what does he want? What does it say, Danni?" asked Gail.

Danni read it out loud. "Hello, Danni. Awesome job tonight bringing forth the Word. Would you be so kind to grace me with your presence for dinner tonight? Love, Bishop Jio."

Gail looked at Danni, and said, "That would be a no. Wait, Danni, why are you smiling like that?"

"Because, girl, I am going to dinner with that man."

"Yes! Wait until I tell Yvonne and Marie."

"Are we going?" asked Ashlee.

"We? Did you get a personal invitation that I don't know about? No ma'am, I'm going on my own."

"Oh, really?" Ashley commented, "You must still be full of the Holy Spirit, because I can't believe you are going out with him. Girl, I am so excited and so proud of you."

"Ashlee, it's just dinner. Please let him know I will accompany him."

After arriving at her suite, her phone rang, and Danni answered.

It was Bishop Puccetti. "I am outside your door waiting for you."

Danni opened the door and Bishop Puccetti stared at her. He couldn't say anything; he was fascinated by her. Danni smiled and knew he liked what he saw.

"Hello again, Bishop Puccetti. Oops, I mean Jio."

"Hello, beautiful." He noticed Marie was with her. He looked at Marie and said, "Marie, she won't need an assistant tonight, okay? I will take good care of her. I promise."

"Oh really? You all think you're grown, huh? Y'all have a lot of nerve leaving me!"

They laughed, and Marie pouted and returned to the suite.

Jiovanni grabbed Danni's hand, and they walked to the elevator. As they stepped into the elevator, a gentleman in a white suit said, "Sir, are you ready?"

"I am now." He looked at Danni, and she looked puzzled.

"Where are we going?"

"You will see, lovely lady."

The elevator door opened, and he escorted her out to a beautiful decorative roof. It was a clear and warm night. The night was crisp and clear. Danni noticed hundreds of stars in the sky shining bright. The roof had blinking lights outlining the only table on the floor.

Jio had arranged for a full jazz band, and as they began to play, Danni smiled at him. He looked at her and returned the smile. Her cheeks were warm from blushing. She wondered if she was out of her league with Jio.

Danni looked around the roof, and said, "This is beautiful."

Smiling at her and still holding her hand, he commented, "You haven't seen anything yet, Danni, and thank you for accepting my dinner invitation."

The waiter placed glasses of Jio's favorite green tea on the table. Jio released Danni's hand and sipped the tea. "This is so good; it just gave me life. This is my favorite drink, and I'm glad you like it.

Danni, your ministry is undoubtedly one of the most powerful anointings I've seen in a long time. It's needed in the end times. I heard you sing before, but tonight when you sang, it sounded like a host of angels standing at attention to usher in the presence of God. You are anointed and funny at the same time. I laughed several times during your sermon. Right after you said something hilarious, you then laid out a profound word!"

Smiling she said, "You think I can do stand up?"

They laughed hard.

"My God, Danni. Your smile is as bright as the moon."

Danni started to blush again and was unable to respond. She tilted her head and smiled at him.

"Are you okay, Danni?'

"Yes, I am, Mr. Puccetti."

"You are being formal again. Ms. Wright, I am captivated by you."

"You have my interest as well, Mr. Puccetti."

"Yes, Lord; look at God." He looked at Danni and he knew this was the beginning of a new journey for them.

They found themselves looking into each other eyes. Danni was nervous and excited at the same time. The thought of him putting so much effort into their evening, made her smile even more. Suddenly, she stopped smiling.

"Hey, what happened to that beautiful smile? What are you thinking about, gorgeous?"

"I am thinking about my past and my present."

Jio stood, took her hand, and assisted her up. He put his arms around her, not knowing how she would respond. He prayed he wasn't being too forward. Danni put her arms around him, and he pulled her close.

"Danni," he barely whispered. "I've had dreams about you before I ever knew of you. I saw your beauty before I ever met you. I heard your heartbeat before I could actually feel it. I asked God who you are and why do I have repetitive dreams about someone unknown to me. God told me, "In His perfect time." He required more time with you. I am here to help remove all of your insecurities, Danni. I feel like I already know you."

She rested her head on his chest. They swayed to the music and were interrupted by the waiter.

"Sir, are you ready to be served?"

"Let me check with the lady. Danni, are we ready to be served?"

She hesitated to respond, because she felt safe in his arms. She finally said, "Yes, we are."

He said, "We can stay right here as long as you want to."

She pulled away from him and looked up into his eyes. Jio moved closer to her face, leaned down, and kissed her cheek.

"Jio," she whispered.

"Yes, love?"

"Um, you smell very nice."

"Thank you, Danni, and you fit perfect in my arms."

"Lord, help me," she said.

The moment was broken and they both started to laugh.

"So, when you're nervous you crack a funny, huh?"

"Yes!"

Jio assisted Danni into her seat, moved his chair close to hers, and sat down. The waiter served lobster bisque soup and a chopped spinach salad.

While they ate, Jio asked, "What do you do, other than evangelize all over the world?"

"I am an investment broker, and you?"

"I manage a Christian magazine."

"Manage? You own the company. You're so humble!"

"I can say the same about you. You are the owner of a brokerage firm."

Laughing, she asked, "How do you know?"

"I read People Magazine and Fortune 500. I am very interested in you, so I did a little research." He laughed, slightly embarrassed to admit that.

"I remember reading about you as well," she said.

"Yes, a few years ago I was featured after my wife passed away."

"Jio, I am so sorry."

"Thank you. Danni, do you have any children?"

"No, I don't. Do you?"

"Yes. I have two amazing sons, Jiovanni and Maximo." Jio removed his cell phone from his pocket and showed Danni pictures of his sons.

"They are very handsome. Maximo looks just like you, and who does Jiovanni look like?"

"He looks exactly like his mother."

"Jio, she must have been beautiful."

"Yes, she was, Danni. Here's a picture of her."

"She was gorgeous! Tell me about her."

"I will, in time, but right now I want to learn about you."

"Welp, as you already know, I'm a Bishop's daughter, the only child. I have four amazing friends, I love theater, I own a business, I'm a preacher with an ex-husband, and that pretty much sums it up."

"Danni, why do you have an ex-husband?"

"He stopped choosing me," she said softly.

"What does that even mean, sweetheart?"

"It means that he cheated on me and is still with the other woman."

Jio notice Danni's mood change, so in order to save the night, he needed to change the subject. "How's your bisque soup?"

"It's one of my favorites, and it's very good. I make a good lobster bisque, too."

"Oh really? How do you have time to cook?"

"I find the time because cooking is one of my passions."

"I hope to experience your cooking one day."

"I'm sure you will."

The waiter removed the soup bowls and salad plates and returned with miso-marinated sea bass with grilled asparagus.

"I hope you are pleased with your entrée, madam."

"Yes, I am. Jio, how did you know I love seafood?"

"I had lunch with a few of your girlfriends today, remember?"

"I'm sure you heard a lot about me, huh?"

"All vital information. As you can see, I listened. How is it?"

"This is really good. I can't eat it all, it's so much. How's your filet mignon?"

"Just the way I like it, medium rare," he replied.

They ate in silence. Jio was watching Danni eat and she looked up to catch him looking at her. She smiled at him.

"Danni, you are so beautiful."

"Thank you, Jio. You are very good looking yourself, but if you keep staring at me, I won't be able to finish eating." Danni couldn't believe she said that.

"Thank you, Danni. I was hoping you were attracted to me."

"Oh, yes I am."

He smiled at her as she finished her fish. "Your friends say you eat really good after you preach." He chuckled.

Laughing, she replied, "I don't eat until after I preach, then I inhale food."

"Do you have room for dessert?"

"No way. I am full, but please, you have dessert. Jio, will you excuse me for a few minutes?"

She got up to go to the restroom. When she returned, she saw Jio speaking to the band leader. The band began to play Ella Fitzgerald's, *All the Things You Are*. The soloist started to sing:

You are the angel glow that lights a star, the dearest things I know are what you are. Someday my loving arms will hold you, and someday I'll know that moment divine, when all things you are, are mine!

"Danni, I haven't been with another woman since my wife passed away, and although this is new for me, it feels good being here with you. I don't want this night to end."

He held her close and kissed her lips.

Chapter Twenty-Five

Charles walked into the Training Room Gym & Spa and noticed so much had changed. Kickboxing, Yoga, Pilates, precision running, spinning, and barre classes were now offered. He walked upstairs to see the spa packages. There were facials, manicures, pedicures, massages, waxing, teeth whitening, eyelash extensions, and microdermabrasion services. The café included organic selections such as smoothies, salads, granola bars, and hot meals. Ice-cold eucalyptus-infused face towels were stacked in mini-fridges scattered throughout the gym. He was glad Danni hadn't removed him from her account. As he walked into the weight room, he saw his homeboy, Tony.

"Hey, Tony. What's up, man?"

"Charles Cox! How have you been man? It's good to see you."

"Man, I'm okay. Getting ready to get my work out on."

"We've been worried about you, boy! You haven't returned any of my phone calls or text messages. What have you been up to?"

"Man, I needed some time to get me together. I got out there too far, but I'm back!"

"Rashad said he saw you and Meghan at Club One a few weeks ago. Y'all still kicking it, huh?"

"No, man. Things didn't work out with Meghan."

"Why?"

"We argued all the time and she started complaining about everything. One time, she had the nerve to call me by her husband's name. Do you know she was still sleeping with her husband after we moved in together? She changed, man. Once we moved in together, she got mean and wanted me to do everything for her. She wanted me to pay for everything. I couldn't take it anymore. Man, I was miserable." He paused and said, "Man, you know what?"

"What?"

"I never stopped thinking about Danni."

"You serious?"

"Yeah, man. I'm getting me together, so I can go to Danni correct. I know I've wronged her, and now I want to right my wrong."

"Wow, man. Have you spoken to her about this?"

"No."

"Do you think Danni wants to reconnect with you?"

"Tony, you know she's always loved me. She has always forgiven me. She's a Christian, remember? Forgiving is the first thing I learned in church, and I know Danni like no other. She loves me. She will give me another chance. You'll see."

"Rashad said he saw Danni and Yvonne a few months ago, and Danni looks good and happy. Well, she's always kept herself together."

"Danni will let me back home, watch and see. Maybe not today, but soon. I even spoke to Bishop Wright a few weeks ago, and I promised him that I would get myself together, so I can get Danni back."

Tony was confused because he knew that Charles and Danni were divorced. Charles had cheated on her and publicly humiliated her. He hoped Charles wasn't having a mental breakdown, because he knew enough about Danni to know that she would not be taking him back. He'd spoken to Danni several times when he saw her in the gym.

"Okay, man. Well, I wish you the best."

"Thanks, my dude. You will see. Let me get started on my workout, and I'll catch up with you later."

Charles worked out, took a shower, and put his clothes on. He sat on the bench, grabbed his phone, and texted Danni.

Hello, Danni. How are you? I need to see you and it's important. Please let me know when we can talk. Thank you. Charles smiled as he finished getting dressed. He grabbed his bag, left the gym, and sat in his car. He looked at his phone to check if Danni had texted him back, but she hadn't. He was getting upset, because he had made several attempts to contact her, but she wasn't responding to him.

He prayed aloud: "Lord, help me be a better me, a better husband for Danni, a good father one day, and a good Christian. I have repented for my sins and I am ready to apologize to Danni. Father, please let her respond to me. If You give me another chance with her, I promise I will treat her like the queen she is. I'll be loyal to her, the way I should have been. I trust You, God. Thank You, Amen."

Charles started his car and drove around the city. He decided to take a ride to Eucalyptus Drive; he wanted to see the beautiful house he'd shared with his wife.

Chapter Twenty-Six

Danni was scheduled to preach at Jio's church, New Life Apostolic Worship Center, in the morning. She'd phoned her friends and her parents, and none of them could attend with her, which was very strange. This was the first time she would travel with only her security team. She pouted because she always had her friends or parents with her, but she knew she would be fine. Her administrative staff had packed everything she needed, so she was ready. She felt like getting out the house and decided to go out to dinner. She locked the house, started her car, and drove to the security gate. She waved to Jake.

Jake said, "Hello, ma'am. I don't show you scheduled to leave this evening. However, I can arrange security for you."

"No, Jake. I can go alone."

"Ma'am, I don't want to alarm you, but I can't allow you to leave alone. Charles Cox is inside the black truck in the cul-de-sac. I will be glad to have a team accompany you."

"I am not interested in speaking to him. Do not let him in."

"No ma'am. I will not allow him inside the compound. I will be glad to chauffeur you wherever you'd like to go after Charles Cox leaves the premises."

"No, it's okay, Jake. I'll stay home."

Danni turned around, parked her car in the garage, and heard Charles yell out her name. She ignored him.

She returned inside her home and was preparing dinner for herself when her phone rang. She looks at it and saw an unknown number; she didn't answer. Danni called Gail and told her Charles had been at her house.

"Do not let him in, Danni. I do not feel good about this," Gail shrieked at her.

"Gail, he won't get in. Charles doesn't want to mess with my security team. It's just weird that he's here. Can you come over?"

"No, Danni. I can't right now. I'm taking care of a business matter, but I will call you after I'm done, okay?"

Feeling abandoned, Danni said, "Okay, I will call you later."

Gail knew Danni was hurt, but she couldn't be there for her at this moment.

Danni's phone rang again; another unknown phone number. This time she answered.

"Hello?"

"Hello, Danni. How are you?"

"I'm sorry, who am I speaking to?"

"Really Danni? It's your husband, Charles."

"Oh! Um, hello, and you mean my ex-husband"

"I miss you, baby."

Danni remained quiet.

"Danni, I made a huge mistake. Please forgive me for the pain I've caused you. I know how bad I hurt you. I returned to Christ, I'm working, and I've gotten myself together."

"Charles, I am glad you are well."

"Danni, I want you back. I have never loved anyone as much as I love you. I told Bishop Wright that you and I have had a thing for each other since we were kids, and I still love you. I was tripping for a while, but I am better now. I can love you the way I should have."

Danni remained quiet as she started to think about everything he had done to her during their marriage.

"Danni, you there?"

"Yes, I'm here."

"Please let me come in so I can hold you, and you can see how serious I am about reconciling."

Danni asked God to help her respond to him the right way. "Charles, I forgive you for all the things you've done to me, and if there is anything that I have done to you during our marriage that caused you any hurt and pain, I am asking you to forgive me."

Charles interrupted her and said, "You didn't do anything wrong, baby. It was all me. Please let me in so we can talk about this face to face."

"No, Charles. That wouldn't be a good idea. I have forgiven you, and I've moved on, just as you have."

"No, Danni." He began to cry. "I've asked God to forgive me for hurting you. I left Meghan because I want you back. I love you, Danni. Please give us another chance, please Danni!"

"I'm sorry, Charles. I am not interested in reconciling with you."

"Please, Danni. How can I prove to you that I'm still that man you fell in love with? I've changed. I'm so much better now."

"Charles, I will pray for your continued success in God. I'm going to hang up now. God bless you."

"No, Danni!"

After she hung up, he cried out loud, then he became angry. Danni could see him from the security monitors in her house. He tried to climb the gate, but he couldn't climb over it. He kicked the gate, but only to hurt himself. Danni saw Jake talking to Charles, and then Stanley, another security guard escorted Charles to his car.

He yelled out, "Danni, it's not over. I'll be back!"

Danni felt sad for Charles, and a little nervous, because she hadn't heard him sound so destitute. Her phone rang again. She looked at it and it said *My Honey*. She answered. "Hi, baby."

"Hello, my love, how are you?" Jio asked.

"I am okay, sweetie, and you?"

"Are you sure? Your voice sounds shaky."

"Yes, I'm sure. How are you?"

Pouting, he said, "I miss you so much, baby. I don't like the miles between us. We are both so busy working in the Kingdom, plus our own businesses. I don't see you enough."

"Yes, honey, remember we talked about this. Wait! Jio, are you changing your mind about us?"

Shocked. Jio asked, "Danni, where did that come from, sweetheart? I love you and only you. I only wished we lived closer."

Danni was quiet. She had gone through so much with Charles, at times she got confused. Jio was a man of quality. He loved her for real.

"Jio, I'm sorry. Baby, please don't make a big deal about what I'm going to say, but Charles came by."

Jio interrupted her. "What? Baby, are you okay? Did you let him in the house? Why didn't you call me?"

Danni smiled because she knew Jio loved her in a way that she'd never experienced before.

"Yes, baby, I'm okay. No, I didn't let him in the house. I didn't have a chance to call you, because you called me right after I hung up with him."

"What did he want?"

"He asked for another chance. He said he has returned to Christ and that he loves me."

His tone changed. "My love, can I call you back?"

"Jio, I don't want him back! I love you, sweetheart."

"I love you more. I will call you back."

"Okay."

Jio ended the call.

Danni wondered what he was thinking. She had to tell him how much she loved him. She texted him. *I love you and only you.*

No response.

Danni phoned him, and her call went to voicemail. She started talking to herself. "Okay, Danni, he's not with anyone else. He is busy doing something and he's not ignoring you. He's not Charles!"

It'd been an hour since she heard from Jio. She reheated her dinner and heard a knock at the door. She knew it must be someone on the safe list with security, because no one could get past security, but everyone on the list wasn't available. She looked at the monitor and saw Ashlee.

She opened the door, and Ashlee said, "Girl, are you okay? Why was he here? What did he want?"

Danni pushed the door closed, but someone pushed it open. It was Jio. She leapt into his arms, and squealed, "Jio, what are you doing here?"

"You sounded so shaken on the phone, I had to be here, love."

She explained what Charles said and reiterated with both of them that she was fine. Jio went outside to speak to the security team and left them with some very strict instructions. When he returned the house, Danni noticed his overnight bag.

She said, "Jio, I thought you had an important meeting for the magazine."

"You are important to me, Danni. When are you going to let that sink into your big head?"

They all laughed.

Ashlee said, "I'm going to my room; you two are making me love sick."

They laughed again.

"If I didn't know you loved me, I definitely know now."

"I am staying here tonight, as well as Ashlee. I need to make sure you are okay, then we will leave in the morning for Malibu. You okay with that?"

"Yes, I am. I have plenty of room for you."

Epilogue

Jio was a major figure in the world of business and a man of God. He was unable to sleep in like most people could. His days started at the crack of dawn, and not one minute later. As he drank his coffee, he began to think about the first few years of starting his business. He was full-time in ministry. His business was his life, and his life was his work. He never dreamed his company would be as lucrative as it had become. He was grateful to God for the vision and how plain He made it, so Jio easily followed His lead.

Today was one of Jio's busiest days. He had a full day of business meetings. He was able to add four more districts in different countries to his magazine publications. Jio scheduled a meeting with his leadership team to discuss contracts and any possible issues that might arise internally. There was always some type of technical issues when acquiring certain licenses for specific applications and compatibilities, but he had the best information technology staff. He wasn't concerned, because he knew that when

212

God led you and you followed Him specifically, He would make your dreams manifest.

He thought about his fiancé, Danni. He smiled as he thought about how beautiful she was and how she'd changed his life. He looked at his watch and knew that she was at the Training Room and Spa, working on her body. He loved her curves that were in all the right places. Jio knew one day God would bless him with his soulmate; however, he never dreamed it would be someone so amazing, creative, and powerful in ministry. She brought balance to his life and he anxiously awaited their nuptials.

He knew Danni had been hurt by her former husband, and because of it, he continued to assist her to understand his honesty, candor, integrity, and the fact that he was a true man of God.

Periodically, when they were together, he would glance at her, she appeared to be miles away. That was when he would embrace her and confirm his love for her. He understood, after a marriage of betrayal, she had trust issues, and he was willing to help her get through those instances.

There was a time in their relationship where she texted him, and he was busy and unable to respond to her text as fast as she felt he should. It was a trigger for her because of her past experiences. To alleviate those times for her, he had an additional phone specifically for her and his children to reach him anytime and anywhere. Although there were times she texted him while in a meeting, he took pleasure in responding to her. It was his company, so he could interrupt business meetings to respond to the woman in his life. He accepted the fact she was still healing, and he wanted to do everything he could to assist her.

As he dressed for the day, he thought about surprising Danni at the gym. He needed some quality time with her. He knew she loved it when he surprised her and showed up where she was at. He thought about the amount of work he had scheduled for the day and decided to stay at the office.

As the team started to assemble in the conference room, Jio got an unnerving feeling that he needed to be with Danni. He phoned her, but there was no answer. He texted her but got no response. He couldn't seem to shake the feeling of discomfort. He wasn't sure where this feeling was coming from.

Jio called the meeting to order and started to discuss the contrasting contracts and pertinent information, so the team could understand the differences in the contracts.

As Jio continued to explain the contracts, he got a feeling of anxiety again. He stopped his meeting to text Danni and ask her if she was okay, but still got no response. He assumed she was working out and didn't have her phone with her. After completing the portion of the contracts with his team, he got a strong need to see Danni. He told his assistant to continue with the agenda since he'd covered what he needed. He also advised her that he was driving to Santa Barbara and reminded her that she knew how to reach him if he was needed.

The drive to Santa Barbara was smooth and easy. He listened to one of Danni's CDs of her singing and preaching. He absolutely loved her and knew that God had His hand in orchestrating their relationship. Jio prayed for years that God would send someone into his life who would enhance what he had going on in ministry, family, and business. He had to wait until Danni could get through her pain with her ex-husband, Charles. Jio thought, *What type of weak and poor excuse of a man can Charles truly be to treat Danni the way he did? He had to be insecure to make her life so miserable.* Jio considered how hurting people often hurt others. He also thought about when Danni told him about how she discovered Charles was cheating on her. He got a little sad, because as sweet and loving as she was, why would a man betray her? If Charles had not cheated on her and sent her through hell, Jio wouldn't be marrying the most beautiful woman in the world.

He pulled into the gym parking lot, saw her car, walked in, and asked the receptionist where he can find Danni. The receptionist knew Danni well and had met Jio several times. She stared at Jio, because he was a very handsome man. Jio smiled at her.

"She's in the sauna, Mr. Puccetti."

"Thank you." He was excited and anticipated the surprised look on Danni's face when she saw him.

Acknowledgments

First, I thank God for being my leader and for protecting and providing for my family and my friends. I am so grateful God chose me to spread His word through preaching and teaching. To my beautiful, amazing, and talented children, Brooke Dannielle (son-in-love, Stanley) Britney Dannielle, and Briajunae Dannielle (Bree); my "other" children, Krystal Keys and Ashli Taylor; my amazing grandchildren, Broq, Suri, and Kennedi—thank you for your tireless support, your unconditional love, your critique (you ladies are so good at it), your feedback, and for hanging in there with me. I love you all, and you are the beats of my heart. Always remember Isaiah 54:17: *No weapon that is formed against thee shall prosper; and every tongue that shall rise against thee in judgment thou shalt condemn. This is the heritage of the servants of the Lord, and their righteousness is of me, saith the Lord.*

To my beautiful sisters: Gwendolyn Gail, Alesia Yvonne (passed away before I completed this book), Pamela Marie, and my brother, James. When Momma passed away, her death took a piece of each of us. Mom didn't teach us how to live without her. I love you all very much and I'm always here.

To my constant encouragers and awesome friends, you know who you are. Thank you for your love, your undying support, and your friendship. I love each one of you. I have the sequel. Can we do it again? LOL!

Dr. Gwen Matthews, (my awesome pastor), Pastor Lisa LaGrone, and Lady Rachelle Benson—thank you all so much for your love, for always pushing me forward, and for having my back! Much love to you all, and may God continue to bless you abundantly!

From the heart of the Author

A Heart That Forgives is for anyone who has experienced emotional hurt, pain, and devastation. It doesn't matter how it happened, when it happened, or who caused it. The bottom line is, it happened. The pain may be so severe it feels as if your heart is disintegrating into tiny pieces. Perhaps, by day you put on a happy face, because things must go on, but then the night comes, and you find yourself lying in bed, tears streaming down your face, and the weight of the hurt heavily pressing on your chest. You wonder if you will ever make it to the other side of the pain, and, worst of all, you feel completely alone. No one truly knows the level of pain the heart can take. When the memories cling to your mind, they numb you and keep you in a dark place, making it impossible to move on. Jesus Christ knew this feeling all too well when He hung on the cross, exposed, beaten, and betrayed by those who loved Him. He felt very alone. His word gives us promises to hold on to when these times come:

The Lord is close to the brokenhearted and saves those who are crushed in spirit. (Psalms 34:18, NIV)

I consider that our present sufferings are not worth comparing with the glory that will be revealed in us. (Romans 8:18 NIV)

For I know the plans I have for you, declares the Lord, plans to prosper you and not harm you, plans to give you hope and a future. (Jeremiah 29:11, NIV)

We are hard pressed on every side, but not crushed; perplexed, but not in despair; persecuted, but not abandoned; struck down but not destroyed. (II Corinthians 4:8, NIV)

If you don't have a prayer life already established, please do yourself a favor, fall on your knees and talk to the only True and Living God, who will help you through the process. You will *need* Christ on this journey.

This is a daily prayer to pray during the journey of betrayal, lies, deceit, and pain:

Abba, help me to accept everything in my life that I cannot control or change. Help me to trust You in the things that are unjust, unacceptable, unfair, and painful beyond words. Lord Jesus, help me let go of my past, so I can begin the process of recreating a future through forgiveness. Help me to know what boundaries to create and give me strength to implement them, in the Name of Jesus.

Lord, please help me focus on what is of good report and the ways I can become better and not bitter. Father, do not allow me to hold any grudges towards the ones who have devastated my life. Destroy the soul tie I have and help me to love those who have despitefully used me. In Jesus' Name, Amen.

.

41624804R00141

Made in the USA
San Bernardino, CA
04 July 2019